Vance

THE McCADE DRAGON BOOK 6

KATHI S. BARTON

This is a work of fiction. Names, characters, places, and incidents are products of the author's imagination or are used fictitiously and are not to be construed as real. Any resemblance to actual events, locations, organizations, or persons, living or dead, is entirely coincidental.

World Castle Publishing, LLC
Pensacola, Florida
Copyright © Kathi S. Barton 2018
Paperback ISBN: 9798891263826
eBook ISBN: 9781629899039
First Edition World Castle Publishing, LLC, March 5, 2018
http://www.worldcastlepublishing.com
Licensing Notes
Cover: Karen Fuller
Editor: Maxine Bringenberg

Table of Contents

Chapter 1

"Where is he?" Morton Elliot, his vice president and right-hand man, said he didn't know, but he'd been at home until an hour ago. "And you saw him? I mean, this isn't a case of him just getting the things out of his body, is it?"

"No. I don't even think he's aware of them, to be honest with you. Yeah, we saw him. I have pictures of him with his brothers. And the markers that are on him were with him every step of the way. I made sure of that myself."

Abe was handed a sheet of paper that meant as much to him as anything else scattered on his desk. It was window dressing. Every note and file, even the fucking pens that had his name on them, were things that people expected him to have on this desk. But it was the desk that he had in his upstairs office, the one that he had the only key to, that was his alone. The desk that had all his businesses, the information on them, as well as everything in the world that he owned and was owed to him. The room that no one, not even his wife, could enter.

There were files and charts in there that would get him put before a firing squad. Things that no president, not even a citizen, should be going over. The country was going to be in for a huge surprise, and he could not wait until they figured it out. President Abe Melton, "Honest Abe," was anything but, nor was he working to help them.

When Morton's watch made a noise, Abe waited for the news. He knew that sound as well as he did the ringtones on his own phone. It was indicating that there was movement. And when Morton sat down hard in the chair, Abe stood up.

"What is it? He showed up, right? Where is he, Morton?" Morton said something, but he didn't understand him. It wasn't mumbled, as it usually was, but a whisper. "What are you saying, you moron? Tell me."

"I said that he's here. In the building." Abe sat down and stared at the door in front of him, expecting it to be slammed open. Being shot was all he could think about. "I'm going down to check on it. You stay put."

"Fuck that shit. I'm going with you." They made their way to the lowest levels in the White House. Few knew about this area, and those that did had more than likely forgotten about it. "When we get there, I want you to show me how to use that machine. I'm sick of not having any idea where he is when I want to know."

"Sure, sure. But if he is indeed in the building, then it'll matter little. We're both dead if we can't get to him first." There was that. "Christ, of all people to still be hanging around."

8

That was true. Vance McCade had been a pain in their asses since Abe had taken office. Before that, really. He was good, too damned good at his job, and it had cost them a lot of sleepless nights as well as a great deal of money. He was just danger. And he was a killer.

The idea to track him with small devices had been Morton's. But he had suggested that they put them on him in all kinds of places. In the event that he lost a leg or an arm, they still wanted to know where he was. Abe didn't think that the loss of a limb would slow him down, so he didn't want to take any chances.

There were only two men that worked this computer, and each did a four-hour shift, never left the area, and were pretty much chained to the desk at all times. Food was brought to them. Their laundry was taken care of for them. And twice a week, someone would take away anything that was considered trash. Even that was gone over so they'd not be sending out any messages. Three times since he'd been in office they'd had to deal with one or both of the employees that had worked in there. Abe thought that with the example they'd made of the previous ones, these two would work out better. At least for their sakes he hoped they did.

"He's all over the fucking place." The blinking lights did seem to be covering the map—the building they were in, outside the grounds, as well as back in his home state of Ohio. Fucking asshole knew.

"McCade is aware of us." Morton said no shit. "Well, Mr. Know-It-All, what the fuck are we going to do about it? It's not like any of your ideas to kill him have worked. He's like a fucking ghost."

"I still have people out looking for that woman. The one that was working for us a long time ago. Seems she's made herself known again." He asked him how. "She killed four of our men in a restaurant a couple of days ago. Actually, two different restaurants. She's as bad as he is when it comes to getting information that we have out there."

"We have to get rid of him. Now." Morton said he was working on it. "Well, work harder. Have you any idea what it's costing us to have him out there?"

They left the little room and made their way up to his offices. Morton was still talking about how they were going to get this woman, but Abe didn't see that working. If she was as good as McCade, then getting her to do anything would be impossible. She'd more than likely turn against them too.

"What makes her so special?" Wording, he was aware, had to be worked around. While he knew there were recording devices everywhere, there wasn't any kind of audio in this room. But that didn't mean that they didn't have them on themselves. "I mean, is she all that special that you want to bring her onboard to work for us?"

"She's said to have a bit of a magical touch that we like to use." So, she was magical, so what? So were most of the men who protected him. "And she has no qualms about using her magic however she sees fit. As I said, she took out four of our men in seconds."

Morton got up and handed him a thumb drive. Putting it in his personal laptop, Abe watched a video of an old woman having a meal. When she stood up two of his men were down, then she and one of them disappeared. He asked where they'd been found, and he got his answer when there were pictures of his man dead.

"Christ. How long was this? I mean, between points A and B?" Morton told him a matter of less than an hour. "He was tracked too?"

"Yes. And she took out another in a restaurant about six hours before. A nice little place that served sandwiches and had free wi-fi. We think that's why he approached her, the idiot. To tell her he knew what she was about. She shot him three times in the gut and just walked out. It's a fucking mess there we had to work hard to contain."

Every day something else was put in his way. All he wanted to do was make a shit load of money, keep his head on his shoulders, and not end up in prison. Abe didn't think that was a lot to ask for. He was president of the free world. Yet every time he turned around, someone was trying their best to take away his freedom. Well, it was time for that shit to stop. And it was going to start by ending that fucking McCade once and for all.

"I want you to find me someone that can bring him to heel. I don't care if you have to go to his mother's house and hog tie her to make him see reason. Also, see if you can get anything on that family. There has to be something somewhere that will make them see reason. Mother fuck, this is the dumbest damned thing that I've run across." Morton reminded him of the cameras in here. "I'd not have to worry about them had you done your job at the house that day. Did we ever figure out what happened to that video? Or even if the pictures we

11

got from them can be cleaned up at all?"

"No. All we know for sure is that one of the women took the drive from our man, but she handed it right back to him. There wouldn't have been any time for her to make any kind of adjustments on it. But all it has on it is fuzz, as well as some audio. Nothing that we can use." Of course not. Why should that be anything different? "Also, the pictures. We did manage to figure out some of that. The camera that was being used by the department there, it was just some old camera. But ours, as you know, are all messed up as well. It's like they— Mother fuck, Abe. Do you think she is magical too?"

"You think?" Christ, he was beginning to hate the world today. "Get her here. I want to talk to the bitch that had a hand in this. In fact, invite the entire clan here. We'll have a nice little get together, and I'll see what I can find out from them. And if I can't find out what I want to know, then we'll have a case of food poisoning that will kill them off and make me deathly ill. Perhaps we can say they brought it, and place the blame squarely in the McCades' laps."

When Morton left him, Abe sat at his desk and thought about all the plans he'd had and how many of them were now shit because of one man. McCade. The things that he'd done and people he'd killed should have had him in jail, but they'd all be counted as justified, and he'd *saved* the American people with each one. There just wasn't any stopping the guy. Not legally, anyway.

Twice he'd had him in his sights. Well, not his own personal sights, but close enough. And in both instances he'd gotten away without a scratch. Abe had been told numerous times that McCade had been shot or killed, and come to find out, the fucker was going home and being repaired there.

Repaired was a strange word, he knew, but they should have been making funeral arrangements instead of patching him up. Abe couldn't even get him for being AWOL, absent without leave, because every time he brought it up to someone, they told him that he was an American treasure and that for as much time as he spent working for the government, a little R&R, rest and relaxation, would go a long way in making him a better man.

"Better man, my ass. He's more of a pain in the ass then even my own kids are most of the time." Abe looked at the picture on his desk, the one of his family taken out in front of this very building. There wasn't any denying that they were a good looking bunch, but Abe hated every single one of them.

Working on his game of solitaire, he thought of all the things he currently had on his plate. There was an arms deal that was just a few days away that would net himself and Morton about ten million apiece. He had a shipment of drugs coming into the country next week that would get them even more cash. Money that he had planned to retire on. As it stood right now, he'd be lucky if he'd be able to run with it. He and Morton both stood to lose a lot if they couldn't get this one man to die.

When his day started, his secretary getting him going to some meetings and shit, he closed up his computer and made sure that the password was in place. There were few that came in here when he was out, but he didn't want anyone to see the shit that he had on it. He'd never make it to the upstairs if they did that. Laughing, Abe went about his morning, but never lost sight of what was really bothering him.

~~~

Vance watched Micky as she worked through the computer. He didn't speak much, but then she didn't either. Just watching her work was a pleasure that he thought he'd not enjoy. Nor had he ever dreamed that they'd be in a house within walking distance of the beach. Looking at the view again, he thought that he could get used to this.

"They're sending out two men to your family home. Your mom's in particular." He asked her why they were doing that. "I'd guess to take them as hostage or some shit. But they're supposedly there to escort them to the White House for a dinner. I've already contacted your brother, Kenton, and he said thanks. He thinks you're the one that warned him, just a heads up."

That was another thing that she did that made him like being around her. She didn't ask him for permission when she did things, not that he thought she would. But she got the job done and did it as well as—even a couple of times better than—he might have. Like today.

They'd split up with the trackers. She was much better at getting places quickly. So, while she was flittering around the country with hers, he was moving around the White House grounds. They really needed better security there, he thought with a laugh.

But he did feel better now that Raven had destroyed the trackers that she'd had. They had shown up on the computer too, the ones that he'd only just found out about. But Micky not only found it, but had hacked into the system, and now they knew as much as the men there did.

"Hey, I was wondering if you had figured it out yet." Vance leaned back on the couch again and asked her what. "That we're mates, or whatever you guys call them. I was a little slow about it, to be honest. It never occurred to me until I was in the shower this morning. When did you figure it out?"

"When I saw you the first time." She nodded as if she'd figured he had. "Do you have a problem with it?"

"No. I mean, you bathe regularly. You don't seem to have any kind of nasty habits that would infuriate me enough to have to kill you, and you're semi-smart." He laughed; he'd been doing that a lot since she'd come around. "You don't do that much, do you? Have a good time, I mean?"

"Are you making an offer?" Her face turned red and he laughed again. "No, I don't usually have any fun. I'm not a fun-loving sort of person."

She nodded. "I didn't think so. And so you know, when you changed your shirt yesterday after coming in from the ocean, I saw the scars. You've had a rough life for someone that is as young as you are." He nodded. Vance had had some close calls since he'd been in the service. "You also have the sword of Caelin. It's meant, I think, to kill his father. You've been chosen to do that. But with all of this, I was wondering what we do now. I mean, a lot is hinging on us being at your family home, isn't it?"

"I don't know how any of this works, to be honest with you, but until this other shit is taken care of, I'd rather not bring it down on them. They — the men that I'm after, with your help — are getting desperate, I think." She said that they were. "I would like to see this through. Not just the thing with Melton, but all his crew too. Then bringing forth the dragon will be a piece of cake, I think."

"Nothing is ever a piece of cake." He just smiled at her. "You want to have sex? I mean, sometime?"

"Yes. All the time." She nodded and leaned back in her own chair. "I'm not forcing you into anything. You want to have sex with me, then I'd suggest you let me know. But I've wanted you since I first saw you, more so when I realized what you are to me. And me to you."

"I'm not sure what I want to do right now. You're kind of scary, aren't you?" He told her that he'd never hurt her. "No, because if you ever tried, you'd be in a world of hurt. Not that I could kill you, but you'd surely wish it."

"I don't want to hurt or kill you. You're kind of scary too." When she grinned at him, Vance felt years of his bad feelings about life in general roll off his shoulders. "I've not told my family that you're here or that you're my mate. I'm worried that if I did they'd want to come here and meet you. Then they'd be in the line of fire too. But soon, we'll have to make an appearance before them. And I want you to know, you think I'm scary? Wait until you meet my sisters-in-law."

"I know Raven. Well, I know of her. I've talked to her before, on a couple of things that I had going on, but nothing face to face. And through working with Jeff, I heard about Emma. She's had it rough too. I knew her brother, Bart. There was a monster if there ever was one." Vance agreed with her. "The others I don't know but have heard about. Your mom, she's a nice person, from the things you've told me about her. Nice, but stern."

"My mom raised us when our dad wasn't around. Pretty much all the time. Then once, when he was pissed off at my mom, he held Lewis down with his boot to his neck and was going to cut his head off. Dad was pissed off because when he'd shown up, again unannounced, there wasn't enough food for him to have a steak. I'd never even had a steak, and he wanted one." Vance thought of that day. "Mom pulled a gun out of her pocket and shot him right between the eyes, like she'd been practicing every day. For all we knew, she might have been. But he was dead, and she had enough proof in the form of hospital visits, as well as police calls, that she got off. I don't think I've ever respected anyone as much as I do my mom because of that."

"I would imagine that she was terrified out of her mind. I mean, killing him, even to save Lewis, she had to wonder what would happen to her sons had she died or ended up in prison for it." Vance told her that she called them her boys. "Boys? I wonder if your mom has had a look at you guys lately. None of you are just boys."

"No. And I'm the only one not married, at least not yet." She didn't say anything, but he felt like he needed to explain. "I'm not trying to make you feel bad. We'll come together, or we won't. But right now we're working together, getting comfortable with each other, and I think that's as good a start as any. Don't you?"

"Yes. But I'm not a pushover. Nor do I want to wait on the man of the house. I don't cook unless I want to. I don't do windows, not even on threat of death, and there isn't any way that I'm going to be the cute little housewife that waits for you with your slippers every night when you come home." He laughed. "I'm not trying to be funny."

"Oh, I know that. I was just trying to picture you with a little white apron on, standing there with my slippers—which I don't own, by the way—waiting for me to tell you to get me a beer. Which I don't drink." He stood up and stretched, and she did as well. "What I would like to see you doing, and this might just be me, I'd love to see you standing in the hallway of our home, naked and ready for me. Where I would take you against the wall, hard and fast, and have you keeping up with me. That's the way I picture you. But for now, I'm going to go take a swim. If you'd like to join me, I'm going to be naked. I don't have a swimsuit either."

He moved out the open doors to the sandy beach beyond. Vance knew that she wouldn't join him. The few times that he'd been in the water since they'd gotten here, she'd stayed on the deck. And when she was in the water, if he joined her, she'd leave the water. Vance wasn't sure why, but he thought perhaps she was as shy about her body as he was his.

The water was warm and calm today. Swimming out as far as he could and still see the house, he decided to float around for a little while, just to try and not think of the woman in the house. She was a conundrum. Beautiful and deadly didn't bother him. It was her shyness that he was puzzled about.

Also, she seemed to have other things about her, magical things, like the porcupine move that he'd not seen as yet. Vance wanted to find out all he could about her, but little of it had to do with her magic, and more to do with the woman beneath it all.

When something touched his skin he thought it was a fish, but turning toward it, he nearly fell back on his ass when Micky was standing not a foot from him, with her breasts bared for him.

"I have a lot of scars. A lot of them are old, but they still are there." He nodded, trying his best to look at her face and not her nakedness. "When I was in the war between the trolls and faeries, I was nearly cut in half. You can still see that scar where I was put back together badly. The magic that was to be mine for helping never came. Not because we lost—we won—but because the troll decided not to share it."

"I've never seen a troll." She nodded. "Are you telling me this because you think I'll think less of you because of them? Or do you want me to know so I can believe how bad assed you are?"

"Both. Neither. I want you to know that I don't show people, men mostly, my body, because I'm not pretty and smooth like most they'd know." He looked at her then, what he could see of her above the water. "Some of the wounds on my body are like yours. Knife wounds. Bullet holes. I have a few that are also from chains around me. Iron has been wrapped around my legs, too, to keep me from being able to run."

"This person who trapped you like that, is he dead?" She said not yet, but she hoped that he'd help her take care of him. "Butler."

"Yes. Because of what I am, what I can do, he thought I

19

was a witch. A person who could help him with his magic. That's one of the reasons that I've been shunned by my kind. My parents, he told them that I did help him and that I had his child. A boy child." Vance told her that Butler could have no male children. "Yes, I found that out as well. But the damage had been done. I had no child by him. Nor did he have sex with me to even create one. Once I was free of him, I was.... It took me a great many years to train myself so that no man would ever touch me again. Not unless I allowed it."

"Are you now? Allowing me to touch you?" Micky didn't so much as blink at him. "I'd never hurt you. Not even it we weren't mates, I'm not a man who harms someone that is smaller or weaker than me unless it's necessary for what I do. You're not either of those, but I have just as much respect for you as a woman as I do my own family."

"I want you, Vance. I do. But don't you feel that we've been manipulated into this?" He started to tell her that he was all right with that when she spoke first. "I like you. I enjoy your company, and you're smart and good to work with. I guess relationships are based on a lot less. So, in answer to your question, yes, I want you to touch me. Make love to me."

Chapter 2

Vance pulled her body to him. He was gentle with her, knowing that while she was strong in so many ways, he didn't want to abuse the simple fact that he was bigger than her. He wanted to kiss her, let her see how much he wanted her, but he didn't. But he did taste her skin.

There was a long scar on her neck that he knew was from a rope burn. He had the same scar on the other side. There was another one under her ear. This one looked like a knife wound. It was smooth except for the stitching that had put it back together.

"Your skin is soft, and you smell of the ocean." Cupping her ass, he felt old wounds there as well, like she'd been beaten with a whip. "I never thought of the ocean as having a smell before. I would have associated it with the smell of fish or gas and oil. You smell like freshness. A little salty, and very warm."

Moving down her body, he took the small morsel of her nipple into his mouth and suckled it. The way it tightened in his mouth made him want more. Lifting her up, he was glad when she wrapped her legs around him, her pussy right at his cock. Moving her enough so that he could fill her, Vance moaned and moved toward the beach.

The sand was hot, almost too hot, so he rolled to his back and sat her atop him. She touched him, brushing her fingers over his own nipples as well as scars that he had on his own body. She asked him how he'd gotten the one near his heart.

"Sniper. And stupidity. I knew he was there, but I thought myself above getting shot and he took me down. If not for the medic that was standing right next to me, I would never have made it beyond my second day." She laughed and leaned down to kiss it. "Who beat you?"

"A lot of different men, and women. Once when I was caught between a mountain and a frozen lake, I thought that I could simply fly over both and be gone before they were the wiser. What I didn't count on was that the queen of a particularly small group of men would be able to send her eagle after me, and he took me down with a whip. Once there, she beat me until the earth helped me heal and I was able to get away." Vance asked if she'd killed her. "Yes, their entire army, with my porcupine skill, as you call it."

They talked and laughed while making love slowly. He was enjoying the stories and the way that Micky rode him by her own set of rules. When he could no longer stand the wait, he rolled her to her back and settled between her thighs. As soon as she wrapped around him, he held her hands above her head and took her breasts in his mouth, one at a time.

"You're very good at this. Like you've had a lot of practice. Have you?" He laughed, thinking what an odd time to find something funny. "And your cock, it's very talented too, isn't it? You make me feel like I'm the only one."

"As you are. As you will always be." Vance touched her every place that he could reach. Touching scars and wounds as much as he did flawless flesh. To him, all of her was perfect. "You are beautiful. To me, you're absolutely beautiful. Your skin is like a soft blanket; your nipples and breasts make me think of pillows laying in the sunshine, and only for me."

"Vance, please. I need to come with you."

He moved deeper into her, letting her hands go so that she could touch him too. Never had he made love with a woman like this. Normally, pressed for time and a need that wouldn't be ignored, he would take a woman where she stood, giving her as much as he got out of it before moving on.

This was the kind of making love that one cherished. And he would. Also the woman. When she cried out that she was coming, he took her mouth and let her scream her release into his body, his soul. And when she came a second time, he emptied himself deep within her until she came again. It was then that she sank her teeth into his throat.

Vance felt the connection immediately. He knew her every hope, her every dream. Even her memories became his. When he came with her the final time, Vance knew a love so profound, so deep that he wondered why he'd never wanted it before. And then he envied his brothers for having had it so much longer than he had.

Holding her in his arms while she slept, Vance rolled to his back, his body spent to the point that he'd not be able to move if someone came for them. Smiling at the thought of loving this woman, he closed his eyes for a moment to let the love that he felt settle over him like the warm sunshine that he had said she was.

Vance woke when she moved off his body. The chill in the air made him realize that he should have thought of taking her in. When she helped him to stand, her body too luscious to ignore, he kissed her deeply and picked her up in his arms to carry into the house. And to bed.

"What if we just stayed here for the rest of our days? I mean, I don't know about you, but I could just leave the world behind." He dropped her on the bed with a bounce, then asked her what they'd do for money. "I own this house. And a few others. I've been around awhile and bought this thing for a song when people didn't have houses on the beach."

"I have a few too. One where my family lives. I've made sure that it's safe for us both." He joined her in the bed, then got up when he realized he was covered in sand. Going out to the deck again, he showered off while still talking to her. "I have one in about every country. Two in Paris. I love it there. My brother Jorden, he has shows there, paintings of his, and we all stay in my house. But now that I think about it, I don't think it's ever come up that I own them."

Drying off, he joined her again on the bed. She was beautiful, and he just couldn't get enough of looking at her. Touching his rough finger to her nipple, he smiled when it puckered. Leaning down, he took it into his mouth and made love to it. She held him there as he enjoyed himself.

Vance. He sat up, knowing that if Kenton was contacting him, something was wrong. *There is something you should know. Nothing bad, I promise, but Emma has been in a car accident. Nothing bad, but it hit the papers.*

What happened? He got up to get dressed, telling Micky what had happened. When Kenton started to laugh, he told her that too. *She did something totally off the wall, didn't she?*

Yes, you could say that. And she's fine, but the other man isn't. And I doubt he'll ever try and take her from her car again. Vance sat down, his knees jelly. *She was coming home from the bakery when this guy knocks at her window of her car. When she only rolled it down about an inch, he told her to do it all the way. Well, you know my Emma, she wasn't having it. So when he smashed in the glass to get to her, she went all macho on him. He has three broken ribs, his face is black and blue, and he has seventy-three stitches on his arms where she clawed him. My wife is a hellion.*

Kenton sounded proud of that. And as Vance relayed the message to Micky, she thought it was funny. Then she asked who had sent them, or did they know yet. Asking Kenton, he thought about telling him about Micky but didn't. Things for them were quiet, and he needed that right now.

Butler, we think. The guy had a picture of the jewelry on him, and that's why we're blaming him. But there isn't anything that he could have done to her, that's my way of thinking about this, so we've banded together and are watching everything. How are things on your end? He told him what had happened today. *I have to tell you, little brother. I can't wait for this to be done so you'll be home all the time. And someday you'll meet your mate. I need you here. We all miss you.*

And I miss you too. I think this will be over soon on my end, then I can come home, provided that I don't end up in prison. They've already killed Samuel. I'm not going to get caught by them if I can help it. Kenton told him he was fine with that. *So am I. I'll be talking to you soon. I have to get going. I have things in the fire here, and I need to make sure that they're still stoked.*

If we can help you in any way, let me know. I want you safe too. And while talking about safe, your house is done. I went over today to have a look at it with Lewis. Damn, you have it set up. I might have you do that for me when you get time. He told him he'd do that. *All right then, be careful.*

When the connection was closed, he looked at Micky. She smiled at him and he wanted to take her back to bed. But they really did need to get this thing done, the sooner the better. When he stood up she did as well, and without saying a word they got dressed and were headed out the door. Time to go visit Honest Abe.

Getting in and out of the place had been easy since the first time he'd gotten in. The sublevels were well guarded, but not enough to keep him out. Two members of the security force had been trained by him, but that didn't mean he stopped for a social time. Instead, he took one out and Micky the other before they had any idea they were around.

The room where the computers were, that was a little trickier. He started to kick the door in, but Micky moved him back and touched the knob, and it came off in her hand. Just pushing it open, she stood back as he entered. He knew, without her saying anything, that she'd watch for others coming and make sure that no one got out until he was finished. The two men in the room just stood up, handed him their weapons, then got down on their knees. He started to ask why when Micky spoke behind him.

"They know who you are." He frowned and wasn't sure that was good. "They're terrified of you. And with good reason. They've had it in their head that you're going to come here soon and kill them, so they wanted to be prepared. The little one in the back, he has your picture over his bunk, so he never forgets what pure evil looks like."

Micky sat down at the computer that was still running. While she did her thing, he watched the two men. He wasn't sure he wanted to be thought of as evil, but he also didn't want them to think he was a pushover.

"You want to live?" Both men nodded. "Then you don't say a word to anyone that we were in here. Got that?"

"Yes, sir. We can do that." The little one looked at the cabinet, then back at Vance before he spoke again. "If you want more information on these pricks, there's a couple of files in there that we've been keeping in the hopes of you coming to get them."

"What sort of information?"

Bing, his name badge said, asked if he could get up. And when Vance told him to go ahead, he opened the cabinet and handed him several manila envelopes. They were not just dated, but also had names on the outside of them.

"When they're not in the room with us, we watch other parts of the house. Most of the things they say, it's got to do with deals they're cooking up. Someone, I really don't know who, put something in the offices and we were able to get to them. When it started printing up what they were saying, we kept it. There are also pictures of other men that have been brought here to be talked to." Vance asked how they'd not gotten caught. "We have all the cameras in the place right here. We just follow then through the building, and when they're headed this way, we clean up."

"You been here long?" Bing told him just over three months. "Then you've been very busy. Why should I believe that this isn't a trap?"

"Because if you really thought we were fucking with you, you'd have killed us by now. At least, I think so." Vance sat down and stared at the two men. "We don't want to be here anymore than you want to be dead. I have a wife and a new baby. Benson here, he has himself a girlfriend. We can't contact them. Not even to say we're all right. I want out of here, and I think the only way that's going to happen is if we're dead or the man upstairs and in charge of this shit is dead. I'm hoping for him dying and not us."

"Me too." Vance asked them about a phone. "I can leave you one here, but I'd not call your wife or girlfriends with any other phone. You do, and they'll be all over your asses. They more than likely have their phones tapped as well."

After leaving them his burner, he and Micky moved toward the stairs. They had to plant a few other devices in the place, then they'd go to the upper floors. Micky assured him that she could get them there, no problem, but Vance was still a little worried. He didn't want to get caught just yet.

~~~

Micky planted the two listening devices under the desk in Elliot's office and two in General Adkins's office. While Vance worked around the oval office, she roamed the halls, watching the people work while they were unaware of her. When someone mentioned a shipment, she went to see what it was about. The invoice said that it was gifts to go overseas, but she had a feeling that it was more than that.

It only took her a second to get the person using the computer to leave her area. After that, since she was signed in, Micky cloned this computer too. That was five now that she had access to, and she was thinking that if this kept up, she was going to need more computers. Just as she was ready to stand up and leave, the computer dinged that a message had come in. Reading it, she sat down again.

"What is it?" She looked up at Vance and was glad now that he'd believed her when she said that no one would see him if he didn't want them to. "You've found something. What is it?"

"There is a shipment of guns being loaded right now on the pier. They're going to be recrafted, then sent out again day after tomorrow. They're going out to sea, where they're going to be picked up on Thursday." He asked her the name of the ship. "The Adkins. Isn't that the name of the general that we just tagged?"

"It is. His family owns a ship yard. All right. We'll see to that now." She told him how she'd cloned the computers. "There's a laptop in the office beyond. But it's password protected. Can you get around that?"

She snorted at him and went to the office. It took her

less time than she thought it would to get in; the moron had written his daily password on the bottom of his calendar. She told Vance that most people did that. Cloning it without looking at anything on it, she closed it and started to put the password back when Vance told her not to.

"He'll know that someone has been— Ah, so you want him to know that someone has been in here. All right. But let's really make this fun and have him shitting bricks. You should leave him a little note saying where his passwords are. Thanking him for making it so easy."

Vance was laughing as he wrote that on the calendar. Then he signed it with his single initial and put a happy face by it. The man was going to be livid when he saw that, and she wished that she could be there to see it.

Two hours later they were at the dock. The ship was there being loaded, and by Army personnel too. That, she thought, was against the law. But then all of this was. Watching them for several minutes, she took out her phone and started taking pictures.

"I'm going to stop this." She asked him what he was going to do. "I'm still in the army last I checked, so I'm going to see what the fuck is going on. Just wait here, in case I need you to come and rescue my ass."

Since she'd seen him in nothing but fatigues, she knew that he'd be able to blend right in with the rest of the men. But that wasn't his style or plan apparently, and as soon as he was close enough for them to make out who he was, Vance raised his rifle up over his head and fired a volley of rounds.

"What the fuck are you doing?" She laughed when several

of the men dropped to their knees with their hands up over their heads. "You all should join them. I'm sure that as soon as the military police get here, they're going to shoot those of you who are not down."

As if they'd gotten their knees cut out from under them, the rest of them dropped. Even the ship captain came out and joined the men. Weapons were tossed away, and after that, he had complete control over them. When she joined him on the dock, he asked her to pull out his phone so he could make a call.

First, he called a friend of his by the sound of it. She could hear him the man's excitement through the connection. He said he'd be right there with his crew, and when Vance ended the call, he winked at her.

"The newspaper." Nodding, she watched him make a second call. "Hello, President Melton. This is Special Forces Sargent Vance McCade. I'm down here at the dock of General Adkins, and I've just made a discovery that you might not be aware of." Vance put it on speaker so that she could hear too.

The president cursed a long streak of words before he seemed to gather himself up. "I'll be down there in a bit. Don't make any more calls, McCade. I don't want this getting out until we have all the facts about those guns."

"I never said they were guns, sir." There was silence at the other end this time. "All I said was I'd made a discovery here. You knew about it, I'm thinking."

"Mother fuck. Why won't you just fucking die?" The line went dead and Vance turned to her.

"He wants you to die? Well, that's just too bad for him,"

she laughed. "I like you just where you are."

Before the president arrived, if he was going to, the local news crew showed up and set up their cameras. She noticed that they were very careful not to get her or Vance in the view, but they did make sure that they got not only the name of the ship, but also the captain, as well as all the men that were on the ground. This wasn't going to play well on the news.

They interviewed several of the men, who had plenty to say about how they'd come to be there. The captain, very helpful in that he was more than likely going to prison, said that he'd been ordered by General Adkins to load the guns onto the ship. And that he'd done this several times before. He even showed them his log book. By the time the president did show up, his name had been bandied around as well, as the man in charge of all that was happening right under their noses.

By dinner time, not only was the president being questioned, but also the vice president and some of their staff. Adkins couldn't be found, but she was sure that he'd turn up sometime soon. She'd make sure of it. And through it all, Vance stood there with his gun on Melton and Elliot. Micky wasn't sure if the man understood that he'd be dead if he moved or if he thought that Vance was protecting him. But then, the man wasn't that stupid. At least she hoped not. She'd never been prouder to be a part of something.

"Mr. President, you say that you were unaware of this going on. Can you tell us how that is possible? The records of the captain of this ship say that you've been here when the paperwork was being signed." Melton looked at her and

Vance but said nothing. You'd have to be a fool to not notice that the man was sweating bullets and pissed off. "There is also information given to us by an unnamed source that says that you were aware of other shipments that have left this dock. What do you have to say to that?"

"I have nothing to say. And if I just happened to be here, it's because General Adkins is a good friend of mine. Or so I thought. I had no idea of his treason to this country. You can bet that if he's found, then I'll have a few questions for him myself." Vance said he would be found, but no one commented. "If there is nothing else, I need to get back to my office. I am trying to run this country, you know, and it won't do that on its own."

"Are you sure about that, sir?" He didn't answer the question but waved the reporter off and headed to his car. "Mr. President, I have more questions for you. There are a lot of drugs coming into the country. Can you tell the people that you're supposed to be protecting what that's all about?"

No answer. When the car drove off, Peter Dillinger turned to them. He looked like he'd just been awarded the Pulitzer Prize as well as a million bucks. He shook their hands twice before he spoke to them.

"He's going down." Vance nodded and said that he hoped so. "Me too. I'm glad you called. And if you need me again, all you have to do is yell. I'm your man."

Vance handed him the envelopes that he'd been given earlier. "Those are conversations, pictures, as well as a couple of people that have been murdered by those two men. Adkins is on his way to a little hangar about four miles from DC. There are a couple of people there that are going to...detain him." Dillinger asked if he could go too. "You'd be better served if you went to his second home. He'll have them take him by there first. Not that they should, but they're going to in the hopes that you'll just happen to be there. This one is just his vacation place, and he'll try his best to pass this off as him not knowing about the activities that are going on here."

"But we have the paperwork." Vance nodded at the man. "You're slick, Vance. I think you should run this country. You'd do a hell of a job, better than we've had of late."

"Nah, I have a dragon to take care of." Peter laughed and walked away. Vance looked at her. "They never believe me when I say that to them. I wonder why not?"

"Perhaps it's your delivery. You might want to work on that." She laughed when he said that he would. Taking her hand in his, he kissed the back of it and they started toward his car. "Where to now? I'm assuming that we have more work to be done."

"Yes. Two more things. One is seeing what Melton has to say once he gets back to his offices. And the second thing, I want to find you a ring. I want you branded with my mark." She felt her body heat up. "You keep that up and I'll be branding you in a different way right here on the dock."

"You can brand me any way you want. Just do it soon, will you?" They were nearly to their car when she paused. There was something here, someone was watching them. "Butler is around here. He might be watching to see what you're doing."

"Let him watch." Vance pulled her into his arms and

kissed her. It was meant to show possession, she knew that, but it warmed her all the way to her toes and back again. When he let her go, she could see the desire on his face. "Okay, we have three things to do today. Back to the house."

Chapter 3

Abe didn't know what to do. Run? That would be the best thing, he thought, but there wasn't much hope of him getting far. Should he just go on like nothing had happened? Like that was going to be able to happen now that McCade had fucked things up for them. Abe looked at Morton when he started cursing.

"That man is going to get us impeached." Abe thought that was a pretty sure bet once this hit the papers. "My wife is going to demand answers too. What the fuck am I supposed to tell her? She has it in her head that I'm running again with you next term. She's enjoying being the wife of the vice president."

"My wife too. First lady is something that she'd had put on her stationary. Not that she mails shit out, but she had it put there." He thought of all the things she had going on too, things that were above board and legal. "Mildred is going to have a cow when she finds out. And I think she'll have no trouble believing it all either."

"Mine too. We're so fucked over this. We need that man dead." Abe told him it wouldn't matter now. They'd dig until they found all the shit on them. "Still, having him dead would make me feel a good deal better." Morton's cell was ringing before he could answer him.

It would be nice for him to be dead, it surely would, but the problem that he saw with that was that he'd be blamed for McCade's death as well. And even though he'd been trying since he took office, the man had never died by his hand. It was like he had nine fucking lives or something.

"I just heard from the computer room. We've been raided." He asked how the fuck that had happened. "Those men we have down there, they called in the MPs. Something about they were told to do it. I didn't tell them, did you?"

"Why the fuck would I have them call in the military police when I have more to lose than you do? Mother fuck balls, I just know it was McCade. Have we heard anything about his family coming here? Not that they would now, but anything at all?" Morton nodded. "Please tell me that their house burned down. Or they've all died from some poison that had them suffering for weeks and weeks. Anything at all."

"The mother called in to thank you for sending her the lovely tea set. She said that it was very nice of you to send her the entire set." Abe counted to ten, then when that didn't calm him down, he counted again. "She is a nice lady."

Abe punched Morton in the face. It might have been a bit

38

more satisfying if not for the fact that he fell forward when the car stopped suddenly, and blood got all over Abe as well. This was why, he'd bet, they weren't supposed to ride in the same car. So they'd not kill each other.

Asking what the fuck was going on, Abe jumped when the door opened to his right. Abe was positive that he didn't want to exit the vehicle. He had no idea why, but he knew that something bad was about to go down. When Vance's face appeared in the empty space where the door had been, he cringed back from him. This wasn't going to end well.

"Hello, gentlemen. I'm to escort you the rest of the way to the White House." Abe said no, but Vance got in the car with them anyway. "Did you know that you both have blood on yourself? And I've not even had my fun yet."

"Are you going to kill us?" That was a good question from Morton. But Abe wasn't sure that he wanted to know the answer. "There are a lot of people that will know that you've done it."

"Of that, I have no doubt. But for now, I'm only taking you back to the White House. Your buddy Adkins has been located. He's been talking like he has one of those strings on him. Pull it and you get all kinds of shit you didn't even ask about." This was bad. Really bad. "You've not asked me why I'm the one escorting you home—well, your home for a little bit longer. Don't you even care? Or is it you've figured it out?"

"I don't want to know." He didn't either, and turned away when Morton asked. He thought it was better to imagine than to know what his fate was. "You've really fucked this up for us, McCade. You could have been a national hero, but now you're going to be shit."

"Oh, I don't know. I did stop a great deal of guns from going out of the country. Where they were headed, they would have killed a lot more men than just me, I think. Then there is the added fact that we found your little room and all the shit that was going on there too." He threw a handful of little devices at them both. Abe knew just what they were. "It was easy enough to figure out who had ordered them put into my body. And I've a good friend who is going over the bodies of my other men that have recently turned up dead. They've found four, so far, in the body of Sawyer."

"If I had a gun...." Abe wasn't sure in that moment if he would have killed himself or McCade. But he seemed to understand and laughed. "You're a bastard, did you know that? A fucking royal pain in my ass too."

"Well, that should be taken care of soon enough, don't you think?" The limo slid to a smooth stop and Abe leaned back and closed his eyes. "No time for napping, I'm afraid. You have a bunch of people here that need some answers. Oh, I'm supposed to let you know that you're also being audited by the IRS. There seems to be a great deal of money in some accounts that have your name on them overseas."

With that, Vance got out of the limo when the door was opened and stood there. Abe thought about running again, hoping that he'd be shot in the head as he did so. It might be a good deal quicker than what he was up against. Everything in his life was going down the toilet.

Every news crew that he'd ever seen was on the front lawn of the White House. Not that they could get much further than they were right now, but he could hear the questions being screamed at him. See the greed in the news reporters' eyes as they hoped for a good shot at him and Morton. Vance was right there, just holding his rifle at his chest like he was going to protect them, when Abe knew that he'd be the first to fire if he could.

Mildred was the first person he saw as soon as he got inside. She wasted no time in slapping him and stomping away. His own wife had turned against him. Not that he wasn't going to get rid of her as soon as he could, but this hurt. She was abandoning her post, which was to stand beside her man. Going to his office, he was escorted by the same men that he'd tried to have killed by sending arms to the countries they were fighting against. Any one of them would have easily killed him, and they'd be justified in it.

Instead of going to the Oval Office, where he thought they were taking him, he was taken to a room he'd had no idea was there — a dark room with mirrors all around it, which were no doubt being monitored by every covert person in the country. Sitting in the room's only chair, he looked at McCade when he joined him.

"Why?" Abe looked at him when he asked the question. "You did this for a reason other than money, didn't you? I mean, please tell me you had another reason for sticking it to the men and women that lay their lives on the line every day for this country."

"You'd like there to be another reason, wouldn't you? Oh, I figure they have enough on me right now that I'll never see the light of day again. So, all right. I'll answer you. No, I didn't have any other reason than to get more money. And who doesn't need more money when it's right there to be had?" Abe looked around the room, at each of the mirrors that reflected back at him. "There isn't a person in this room with us that wouldn't have done the same thing. You too, if given the chance."

"No, I'd never do that." Abe nodded, but didn't agree or disagree with him. "You had it all, you know. A good job, safe from anyone trying to murder you, and you fucked everyone over for money. I think you're the saddest person I've ever come across."

"Me too now that I'm caught. I don't want to talk to you anymore, McCade. You've done enough damage to me for one lifetime." McCade didn't say anything then, which was good. Abe was trying to figure out his own fate in all this.

"Mr. Melton?" He nodded and noticed that he was no longer Mr. President. "My name is Agent Oliver Stanton. I'm from the Federal Bureau of Investigation. I'm here to ask you some questions about some things that we've been made aware of." Abe said that he didn't want McCade there. "Well, that's just too bad. I want him here, as do the rest of the people that are here to ask you some questions. I don't care if you're comfortable, but if you want a drink or something, I can get you that. It's going to be a long day."

"No, I'm fine." Abe looked at McCade. If they ever wanted to update their recruiting posters, this man would be the best one for the job. He was every bit military, from the top of his buzz haircut to the bottom of his boots. His appearance just screamed don't fuck with me. "Let's get this over with, shall we? I have a country to run into the ground."

Abe laughed but neither man did. He was in over his head, they all had to know that. So if he was just a little insane at the moment, that was the reason why. As the questions started coming, mostly about the arms deals he had set up, one thought kept coming to his mind. He wondered what was going to happen to McCade now.

They'd have a parade in his honor. Then almost as he thought of that, he discarded it. He'd not want that. It would be showy, and this man was not. He'd like something like a nice dinner with just him and a woman. No one knowing his name. McCade wasn't going to go far with that way of thinking, but Abe thought he was right. That was just what the man would want.

The questioning went on for six hours. He answered them honestly, or as best he could, giving up the names of the people that he'd had on his payroll, as well as a couple he wished had been. There was no point in lying to them. When he'd started out doing just that, they had brought out paperwork, his own words on a transcript that proved him wrong.

Abe thought he was finished for the day when Stanton said he was finished for now. All he wanted to do was go to his rooms, take a long shower, and lie down. But he knew that wasn't going to happen when two men came in, handcuffed him with his hands behind him, and took him to the van waiting on the front lawn. He was going to prison, just as surely as he'd gotten out of bed that morning.

This time McCade didn't go with him. He was at the

prison when he got there, but he neither said anything nor looked at him directly. Abe supposed he'd seen and heard enough for one day, and wondered what the man was going to do now that his mission to ruin him was finished.

"Fucker."

The men that were taking him to his cell looked at him, but he only told them that he was talking to himself. Sitting on the tiny little cot that was going to be his bed for a while, he held his belongings and tried to empty his mind.

He'd woken this morning as President of the United States, and now here he was, sitting in a jail cell with one tiny window, a cot, and a toilet that hung on the wall. "And now, because of some hotshot Army boy, not only am I going to go to prison for the rest of my life, I've lost everything to boot." Abe wondered where his wife was right now. "Packing what she can to get out of the place. And she won't even think to get me a couple of pens with my name on them either. Ungrateful bitch. Who did she think he was doing this for?"

Well, it was for him, but she didn't have to know that. But like a lot of things of late, he was sure that she knew she wasn't going to be in the picture for much longer than it took him to call in a favor and have her killed. Being the president and having a wife killed while they were vacationing would have gotten him a lot of votes too.

Abe lay down on the lumpy cot. He didn't know what was going to happen tomorrow and really didn't care, but for now, he was going to think. Closing his eyes, he closed his mind too. There wasn't anything to think about, as far as he was concerned.

~~~

The trip home was quiet. Vance had a lot on his mind, and he was glad that Micky seemed to understand. They might have stayed for a couple of more days had it not been for the newspaper people, as well as the news reporters, hounding them everywhere they went. He was just glad that they'd been able to keep their residence location out of the news so that they could return there when this quieted down.

"Sergeant McCade?" He looked at the stewardess that had been tending to the needs of those in first class with them. "There's a phone call for you. It's been patched through on the air phone. Can you take it?"

"Yes, ma'am. Thank you." He knew that it wasn't his family. They were aware that he was coming home. And if they wanted to talk to him, a phone wouldn't be the way they'd go. So whoever this was, they were calling with bad news.

"Don't be such a pessimist. It could be good news." He asked Micky why they'd not just wait until he landed then. "I don't know, but maybe they were just so excited to tell you that you've won the lottery that they couldn't wait."

"And since when are you an optimist, thinking that I won something like the lottery?"

"I'm not, but I hate to see you upset." He picked up the phone when it was brought to him. "Just don't kill anyone if it is bad news."

"I'll try not to."

He said hello into the receiver and heard nothing in return. He started to tell the woman who had brought him the phone when he heard someone laughing. It was Speaker of the House Kirk Delaney.

"Sergeant Vance McCade? This is Acting President Kirk Delaney. I called to thank you on behalf of the American country." Vance told him he'd had a lot of help. "Yes, I've heard that as well. We lost a lot of good people in this. And I'm to understand that you have a wife that you're taking home to meet the family."

"She's not my wife just yet. I've asked her, but she's not had a good chance to answer me yet." He winked at Micky when she slapped him on the arm. "But yes, sir, I've gotten permission to take some time off. And to see to something at home."

"I heard that as well. You're a good man, McCade. Thank you." There was a little shuffling going on and he heard laughter again. "I have a mess here that I'm sure.... Well, I was going to say that you'd not believe, but I just bet you can. I'm working my way through this slowly. It's only been half a day, but we don't want the American people to think that we've totally let them down."

"No, sir. I can see that happening." He wondered what Delaney wanted and started to ask, but he started talking again.

"I was wondering if you could come back here and talk to me as soon as you're done with the things at home." Vance said he'd be glad to talk to him. "Bring your family. I'm to understand that there was some trouble that was going to have your family brought here under less than good intentions. I assure you, young man, I have nothing but praise for you, and for your family for raising a good man."

"I'll have to ask them, sir. I don't spend a lot of time at home lately, so I don't know what they have planned." Vance held onto Micky's hand tightly. This was too surreal. "My mom, she's the head of the household, no matter how old we are. She'll be the one that needs to say yes or no."

"Good man. Yes, you ask her, and when you have the time set up, you give me a call. I'll make sure that you have a direct number to me. Also, one more thing; when this is all finished here, with Elliot, Melton, and the others, I'd like to talk to you about some other things. You have a good head on your shoulders, and I want to see if I can get you to come and work for me on a more permanent basis." He told him he was about ready to retire. "Well, we'll talk about that as well. Or maybe I'll speak to that mom of yours. You call me, son. We'll work it out."

After ending the call, he looked at Micky, telling her quietly everything that he'd said to him. She asked him what his plans were. Vance told her that he didn't really have any, other than to be with her.

"I don't want to think of anything beyond this thing with Butler. He's enough for us right now. Whether or not you work for the government again, that would be up to you. But for now, I think I just want to meet your family, rest up, and try to make some sense of how this is going down." He asked her about the jewelry and if she knew anything about it. "Nothing other than what everyone knows was there that night. The necklace was left behind, and it's not been seen since."

47

"Raven has it." She looked at him. "She took it from him the night that he made her his slave and he killed her mother. Butler thinks he's had it since that night too. But he only has a copy of it, not the real thing."

"Do you know what that means?" He told her that he thought they were ahead of the game. "Not only that, but you can call the dragon without him even being aware of it. I have to look into a few things, but I'm sure that it should end as soon as he's called."

"I doubt if it'll be that easy, don't you? I mean, in my experience, usually things that look easy and sound that way are far from it." Micky said she had to do some research when she got herself a computer. "Yes, me too. I have to see if I can find someplace that I can hide away with you for a while. I was thinking a few months of nothing but us having sex all the time."

"You have a lot of confidence in yourself there, big boy. What are you going to take to make this happen? I've a few tricks up my sleeve to help you should you want to try."

Vance laughed. "I think you might just kill me without any magic. You're almost too much for me."

They were laughing when the pilot told them they were ten minutes out. Gathering up what they'd brought with them, which wasn't all that much, he was happy to be home. And to see his brother when he picked them up.

Lewis had said he'd be there, and he was glad it was him. He didn't want to overwhelm Micky with his family right off the bat. They were too much for most people. But like him, she'd been alone for a long time, and he didn't want her to turn them into ducks or something.

Getting off the plane, he saw them all. Shaking his head, he decided not to warn either of them. They were all on their own with this one.

His mom was the first to hug him. She gave the best hugs in the world, and Vance couldn't help but hold her a little more when she started to let him go. Then he hugged his brothers, all of them giving him a hardy pat on the back that was meant to make him stagger a little. He was made of sterner stuff than that.

"Everyone, I'd like you to meet my mate, Micky Oliver McCade. She came to help me when Caelin sent her."

No one moved, nor did they say anything to her. He started to tell them to get their heads out of their asses when Raven came forward first.

"I'm glad to finally meet you, Micky. I've talked to you so much over the years. It's nice to have a face to go with your voice." She thanked her and then Emma moved to the front. "This is my sister-in-law, Emma. You and she have a mutual friend as well. Jeff."

"Yes, he's told me all about you. He's slightly in love with you, I think." Emma laughed and said he was like her little brother. "Yes, he is a good man."

Mom hugged Micky next and then looked her in the eyes. Vance wondered if she was looking for some kind of flaw. When she turned to him, he could see the tears that sprinkled over her cheeks, and told her not to cry.

"She's everything I hoped that you'd find in a mate, Vance. And so lovely. What are you dear, if you don't mind me asking? Military, or just bad assed?" Micky told her that she was a little of both. "I'm betting more of the bad assed than anything. You'll fit right in with the rest of them. Welcome to the family."

As they made their way to his mom's home, Micky told them how she'd ended up helping him. He looked out the window, seeing the town that he'd grown up in and been away from for far too long. The visits were nice, but he was glad to be home now.

"We've read about what happened in Washington. They never mentioned either of you by name, but then I get this very nice call from Acting President Delaney. He invited us all to the White House for a dinner." Vance groaned and said that he was going to talk to her about that. "Yes, I'm sure you were. But we're going, even if I have to drag you there by your ear. You tell him, Micky, that he is going."

"I don't think I should be the one to do that. I don't have any plans of going either." Mom smacked her on the leg and said she'd work on them both. "I don't even own a nice dress. What on earth does one wear to that sort of thing, when jeans are all I've worn for most of my life?"

"We'll fix you up. I'll have the girls go with us when we go shopping. I'm quite the shopper, so you know. I can find a deal like it's my job."

Vance was still laughing when they were in the driveway. His mom would have them convinced to go, even if she had to have them there at gun point. Vance was wondering if he should get his uniform out and get it cleaned when they pulled up in front of the house. It was good to be home.

Chapter 4

Jorden worked until his hand cramped up. It was nearly finished, and he was excited to see it complete. Just last week he'd been working on it, stepped back from the family portrait, and was startled that instead of his brothers that had their mates, they were their dragons. But when he looked again, it was just the men he'd grown up with and not their other halves. Today, his plan had been to put Vance in, with Micky.

My lord. Jorden paused in his painting to wait for Warrior to speak again. *The young lady that is with Lord Vance. She has not put the necklace on as yet. I cannot speak to her or see if I can help her.*

"I think that they're resting. And knowing you like we all do, we figured that they'd get no rest like they need if you were talking to them." He said that he'd not bother them too much. "That's the point, Warrior. They don't want to be bothered by anyone. My brother has been on the go for a very long time. And last night when he was having dinner with us, I could see the fatigue that was all over his body. The two of them have worked very hard this past week in getting the country back to something safe for us all. Just let them rest, okay?"

I should have been better prepared for them. Jorden told him that they'd not known about Micky either until they arrived. *She is well then? The young lady?*

"She's not young. Beautiful, yes, but she's as old as Raven and Caelin, I think. Might even be older." Warrior said nothing, but Jorden knew that he was far from finished talking. "You know her?"

Nay, I do not. But then, I only knew some of the people in the castle. I was hidden away, much like young Caelin was. Jorden had figured that. *I will wait, but I should tell you that Butler is making plans to come here soon. And will be arriving even sooner now that all the women are here. He will think that he has only to come and call to the dragon.*

"We've been talking about that as well. I think we'll be just fine." Warrior said of that he had no doubt. "Once they are rested and well enough to get up and around, then we'll all sit down and figure out the completed plan for getting rid of Butler. Did you ever find out how much longer he has on his magic? I know that you mentioned once that his is depleting. Is it still?"

It was something that had been brought up a few days ago—that the magic Butler had was wearing off. He might be able to sustain himself with magic that he could take from anger, something that most people with black magic could do, but it wouldn't stay with him for very long. Raven was working on keeping others like her, witches with both kinds of magic, out of his view so that no one else could get hurt.

He is no longer using it to keep himself well, but I believe he is banking it, I believe it is called, for when he comes to you. When I last felt him on the earth, I could feel his weakness, as well as that he is very sick. Black magic must be maintained, and he is doing nothing to do that. I would say that once he is here, he'll show himself to be well, but you'll be able to see his faults too. Jorden thanked him for that. *Nay, you all have that ability now. And more magic than you did before. With Micky being here, you have received a great deal of faerie magic. She is very powerful. I just didn't know where it was coming from until now.*

"I'll have to thank her for the things she's sharing with us. It might be helpful to practice a little before Butler gets here." He felt Warrior's hesitation and wondered if it was just him or the dragon was worried. "What is it, Warrior? Something that I can help you with?"

If he gets to any of the women, especially Micky, if she is indeed the source of the extra magic, he'll drain her to have more magic to hurt you with. She will be able to replenish it, but it will take her some time. I would like to suggest that you put in supplies for her. She'll need fresh fruit, and juices from those and fresh vegetables. And greens. Like lettuce and other things that come from the garden. He asked about red meats. *She can eat them, but the others will be more helpful. She should be able to store extra magic in it as well, if she is as old as you think.*

He made a mental note to make sure that all the houses had what she'd need. When Warrior said that he'd come back to him later, Jorden told him he was there for him. Putting his painting away and pulling out a new canvas, he thought of the dragon, the one that he'd seen in his dreams.

He wasn't as large as he'd thought he'd be. Nothing like the size of the one that was now living at Lewis's home. But he was beyond beautiful. His scales were blue, of course, but not a single color. He could see so many different shades of blue that it boggled his mind to try and come up with ways to paint them. Jorden was sketching the likeness on the canvas when he saw him again, this time nearly on the cloth he was working with.

"You will allow them to hang this in the castle."

He knew the beautiful woman that had joined him. She wasn't here, he supposed, but he had spoken to her on other occasions. Jorden told her that he'd be honored to have it there.

"You will see so many paintings when you are all there. I have hidden them away for your family."

"You're stronger now, aren't you?" She nodded at him and asked to see the other painting he was working on. He pulled it out for her. "I see dragons there sometimes. I didn't paint them, yet they look just like my family's dragons."

"That is the magic. And the likeness of them all, it's very good too. You are going to give this to your mother?" Jorden told her that was his plan. "She will love it. I think her to be a strong woman, your mother. She will make a good queen."

"I don't think she thinks so. She's told me, when it comes up, that she thinks that it should be Emma, not her." Prisane nodded but didn't say anything as she looked at his painting.

54

"Why is she the queen and not Emma? She's Kenton's wife."

"Because without her there would be no dragons to save us all." She smiled at him. "Emma will be a queen soon enough, when your mother decides that she no longer wishes to do so. I'd not tell her that as yet. You will know the time better than most. You have a good eye for people."

"Thank you. But she might be upset when she hears it. Are you going to make sure that I'm safe?" Prisane laughed with him. "Warrior is worried about our newest member to the family. Her name is Micky. She's a faerie, and has not put the necklace on yet to suit him."

"Warrior was always a worrier. When you have finished with the painting, what will you do as a background? I would like to show you the castle from my days. It will be ready soon, and I think it a nice place for you all to be while you get to know everyone. And you can all rest too." He asked her what she meant. "It's time that you go there, all of you. And I'll make sure that Butler is there too, when the time is right. But he'll come, as soon as he feels the magic there."

"I thought we'd take care of him here." She shook her head. "All right. I'll make the arrangements for us to go there. And—"

"The castle has been readied for you all. Everything you need, servants as well as clothing, has been provided. Go there soon, please. There is much that I would wish that you'd do before Butler arrives. And the young miss, yes, I know Micky. Have her put my necklace on when she gets there. Nothing will make him go there but that, I think. Not even me telling him that you are all there." He asked her if any of them would be in danger. "No, not any more. You are as safe as I could make you."

When she left him there, he sat down and tried to think what reason they had to go to the castle to take care of Butler. From what he'd heard about the place it was nearly nothing but stone and rocks. And he didn't understand how it had been prepared for them. Did that mean there was a hotel close to it for them? Whatever it was, he would tell his family tonight, and hope they would all agree to this without too many questions because he didn't have any answers to give them.

Jorden worked for another three hours. He was always amazed at how quickly time went by when he was up in his area working. He noticed that while he was in his own zone, at some point Harper had joined him and was working at her wheel.

"You've been busy." She said that she needed to think. "Yes, that's what I wanted to do too. But I've had several conversations with people that aren't here."

"Warrior? He contacted me earlier this morning. But I couldn't talk to him then. He's worried about Micky." He told her that he'd calmed him about it. "Who else?"

Jorden told her about the visit from the queen and how she wanted them all to go to the castle. She seemed to be excited about that almost as much as he was dreading telling his family. After telling her what he thought was going to happen, she laughed at him.

"I think you're going to be in for a big surprise. They've been talking about going there for a few days now. Mostly after this thing with Butler is completed. But going there to end this, I can see why that would be important." He told her that he couldn't. "Sure. We end it where it started on the very ground that Caelin lived, and the queen lost her throne. It'll be poetic, for all of us. And if the castle isn't finished, I'm sure that she'll fix it so we will have a lovely stay while there. Heck, I might even do some major shopping, if we have some time. I'll need things for the new babies."

Jorden thought of all the things he could do too. Seeing the castle would be fun, no matter what sort of shape it was in. To get away for a while, in a new place, would be nice for them all. And Gavin would dearly love it. He'd been looking up things about the area for months now. Jasmine might even find herself an antique or two to bring home as a treasure.

"Okay, I'm sold, but you have to go with me to tell the rest of them. That way, if they have questions about the trip, you can tell them how much fun it'll be as a distraction." She told him she'd do it. "Great. I'm going to see if we can meet at Dragon's Lair and make plans. She said the sooner the better with this. And Micky isn't to wear the necklace until we're there."

"Yes, from what I've read about it, once all the pieces are on us, then the magic will be great. And I'm betting Butler will want to know what the fuck is going on with that." Jorden said he could not wait to no longer worry about the man. "You and me both. I just want to have a few days where we don't have to be looking over our shoulders all the time."

That would be nice. As he started cleaning up his brushes he thought of things he'd like to do once there was no more threat of Butler. He was going to take his growing family on a long trip. Perhaps rent one of those big campers and see the country. Then they could do the same in other countries as well. Just be a family with nothing but time on their hands.

The table was set for them when he got to the Lair. Lewis was talking to one of his employees about an upcoming wedding, so he wandered around the kitchen looking for something to munch on. He'd missed lunch again and was starving. As soon as he spotted the desserts he made a bee line toward them, but was thwarted when Lewis caught him.

"Don't touch them." Jorden pouted. "That won't work on me. You have no idea how much time we have in those suckers. They're for a wedding party tomorrow. And if they have nibble marks in them, I might not get the job. And I want this one." Jorden asked who it was for. "Mark Pranks. You've heard of him, haven't you?"

"The software designer?" Lewis said that was him. "I had no idea he was getting married. When did he contact you?"

"He didn't. He got in touch with Gabe, who he knows well. She set his arm or something when he'd fallen while drunk. I guess he didn't want the papers to find out he had a slip and she fixed him right up. But she recommended us to him, and I really would like to do it." Jorden backed from the desserts and went to the dining room with the promise of food. "You really should try and eat a meal when you're working."

"I forget. Besides, you do the same thing."

They were laughing and teasing each other when the rest of the family showed up. Jorden kissed his mom and his wife, and they were joined by Gavin when he got out of school. As soon as everyone was seated and had a drink, Harper told them what was going on. He could have kissed her too.

~~~

"So, we're going now instead of when all this is finished." Vance had only been up a couple of hours when his mom had called. "I don't know. This seems sort of risky, don't you think? There is no pack that we can depend on. The security in any place that we stay isn't going to be up to what I think we'll need. I don't have any place I can get any kind of weapons, and while I don't think that they'll work, I'd feel a good deal better with something on me when I face this guy."

"You won't need any weapons." Caelin, who had been absent as late, joined them in the room. Vance was always amazed when he came around. He didn't look any older than any of them, nor did he seem to be anything but a young man. "I've been to the castle today, just before coming here as a matter of fact. And it's done for the most part. There are a few things that it'll need, but I'm willing to bet that none of you will notice it when you get there. It also has all the comforts of a home built by today's standards."

"You mean Internet and phones." Caelin nodded at him as he took a seat at the table with them. "You're here. I mean, not like your mom—you're actually in the room with us."

"I am. And should you share some of the delights at this table, I would be most happy. My wife is with my granddaughter; she's just birthed a baby boy for us all." After everyone congratulated him, Caelin looked at Vance. "You are still unsure about this, aren't you?"

59

"I am. We know nothing about this place, nor the people there. For all we know, this could be an ambush and you and your mother aren't really visiting us. I don't like this at all." Caelin said it was fine when his mother hushed Vance. "I've been somewhat of a warrior all my life, and I can't just turn it off because you say that we're going to be safe when we get there."

"I do understand that you're uncomfortable. If you can think of any way that I can make this transition easier for you, I'd gladly do it. Your family is correct about going to end this where it all started. The magic, for you and your family, will be stronger there. My father's will as well, but he is so depleted now that it will make little difference. I promise you, with all the jewelry, you have all that you need to make him suffer. And he will."

"Suffer for what he did to you and your family. But what about ours?" Vance looked around the room, remembering everything that had happened to each of them in order to gather the jewelry up for this cause. "All of us in some way have been hurt by this. The women here, they've given up their lives to be here. While it might be better for them, it's been pointed out to me that we've been manipulated into this. The wives of all of us were preordained to bring us the magic."

"You would have met them anyway, Vance. They were your mates from the beginning of time. I understand you have no reason to believe me when I say that I am profoundly sorry for what you've all endured. But I can promise you this—when this is finished, and there is no other outcome for it now, you will have riches beyond all imagination." Vance told him he had no use for more money, that he had all he needed. "The riches that you all are to receive aren't just money. There is some, a great deal of it as a matter of fact, but there will be magic, more than enough to keep your family and the people that work for you happy and safe. As you've come to understand too, money will bring its own set of problems. Sadly, that's how the world works. But no one will be harmed again. Not even a scratch that won't heal immediately no matter what."

"How can you make that happen?" Caelin stood up and put both his hands on the table. Vance was sure that he was mad, that he was going to toss the table and all the things on it to the wall, but he didn't. But the table took on the shape and look of a map. "Where is this?"

"Where the castle is." The castle was zoomed in on and he could see that it was indeed finished. The lakes surrounding it were wide and blue, the grass and trees as green and full of fruit as any he'd seen around here. "See the mountain there, is at the back of the castle? It has trolls living in it. There are also faeries that help with the plants and fruit. Brownies live along the waterways. Even the animals that live in the lakes and ponds, they are there only to serve you and this family."

"Look at the wall there, Uncle Vance. I think that getting over that would be hard to do, don't you?" He nodded at Gavin, who was looking at the map from all angles, like he was trying to memorize it for future use. "There are houses here, along the lake. Who lives in those?"

"Pack. But not of wolves like you have here. There are

many there, watching for someone to come along that doesn't belong. Reindeer and water buffalo are in those houses because of the proximity to the water. There are also llamas and horses. We have winged horses, as well as unicorns that lend to the magic. And of course, a few dragons." Vance was beginning to see that they were prepared to take on the former king. "There on the lands is also a swordsman. He and his family have been forging swords since I was a child. The one that you have now, it was made by his family."

"And they'll stand with us? All these people and animals, they'll stand with us when Butler comes?" Caelin said that they were happy to stand with the McCade dragons again. "I'm feeling better about this, but not one-hundred percent. I'm sure you can understand my nervousness."

"I can, and I applaud you for it. Had it not been something that the sword knew about you, then it wouldn't have gone to you when you were ready." Vance felt it move along his back when Caelin laughed a little. "The time for you to practice with it is soon, Vance. You will know how to use it, thanks greatly to the memories from the brooch. Also, when the necklace is put upon Micky's throat, you will have the armor of a man ready for battle. And you will be as ready as you can be, this I promise you."

It was decided that they'd leave the day after tomorrow. The houses had to be closed up, and arrangements made for mail and plants. And Lewis had to find someone to run the restaurant while he was gone. Things that were every day for them, but as foreign to Vance as anything he'd ever done.

Vance went to see his mom when Micky said she wanted

to see about getting herself some clothing to take. Caelin told them that the weather was nice, a warm seventy-five degrees. As soon as she left with the other women, he decided it was high time he spoke to his mom. She would have the answers that he needed.

"You going to marry her before you leave?" Vance laughed; his mother was nothing if not right on point. "You should wait and do it in the castle. I'm sure that we can have it all arranged somehow."

"Actually, that's what I wanted to talk to you about. I don't want to give her a wedding band. Neither of us are the type of person that wears a ring, and it could be dangerous in our line of work. But I would like to marry her by encircling her with the necklace. I think that would be just as good, don't you?" She kissed him on the cheek and told him that was very romantic. "Yes, well, I do have my moments. Thanks to you."

"I can make some arrangements for you before we get there. I was given an email address of the butler there. Do you suppose that Grady and Harper will stay there after we're finished?" He hadn't thought of that, having his family not all here. "I guess it was bound to happen someday, that you'd all move away and leave me here all alone."

"Wow, that was pitiful. How long did you practice that before bringing out the big guns?" She laughed with him. "If it makes you feel any better, I'm not going anywhere. Unless it's for short trips. The new president asked me to come and talk to him, all of us really. But I'm not going to work for him. I'm done."

"Yes, I've heard that said before. Not from you, but I've

heard it. You'll do what you need to do, and I'll love you anyway." Vance hugged his mom and didn't let her go for several minutes. "I've missed this about you. The way you hug like it's the last one I'll ever get. I used to be worried about it, but knowing that you can't get killed makes me enjoy them all the more."

"I love you, Mom. And I have to tell you something. All the times that I was gone, I never forgot what you told me when I left the first time. You told me that I'd better come home when I could, and when I was here, I was here. You also said that when I was over there, away from all of you, that I'd better be there and not thinking of anything but coming home to you. I thought of that with ever mission I was on."

"I love you, son. And I'm so glad that you found someone like Micky. She's like you, but not too. You're very...well, strong. Strong willed. Strong of mind and body. While she's soft when she needs to be. Keeps you in line and happy too. I couldn't have asked for better daughters than the six I have."

Having lunch with his mom was fun. She had the cook make his favorite meal and they talked about the upcoming trip. She wasn't going to think why they were there, but that it was going to be a vacation of sorts. Vance thought that his mother was fibbing to him, that there was nothing else on her mind but dealing with Butler.

When he went home, he started throwing things in his duffle. He'd never owned a suitcase before, so thought nothing of using what he'd always used. When Micky came home with only two bags, he asked her if she was having the rest sent here.

"No. And remind me to never go shopping with them again." He laughed. "I kid you not, Vance, they're like mad women when there's a sale. And they couldn't believe that I only wanted a couple of pairs of jeans and some underwear. It was like I'd caused some sort of space warp or something. And that Jasmine, she's fucking scary when she figures out that something has been marked up before being marked down. Christ, I thought the guy that was helping her was going to bawl his eyes out before she was finished with him."

"What did he do to make her happy?" She glared at him and said he was missing the point. "No, I think that she was justified in wanting answers. I don't think she needed to make him cry, but did she get the sale price?"

"No. They gave it to her, for pointing out the mistake on the store's fault. I would have given it to her too. Just to shut her up." She tossed her jeans onto the bed with her underwear. "Apparently those aren't underwear that I put on, but panties. What the fuck difference does it make what you call them? They fit, hold the right things together, and I'm not catching myself in the zipper pulling on my pants."

"Yes, that's why I never go commando anymore. It's painful to catch yourself in the teeth of death." They were both laughing when he told her what his mom had said about moving away. "She nearly had me there until she pouted. While she was adorable when she did it, she isn't the pouty type."

"Your mom told me that she thinks I'm perfect. I didn't know what she meant until we were shopping. Emma said that I was perfect for you. That still made no sense to me until

Raven told me that even though we're mates, she thought that—with us being so…like, you know, bad assed—we were perfect for each other. Am I all that bad assed, you think?" He nodded. "Well, I hope that someone also notices that I'm good at fishing, as well as being a good housekeeper."

"Housekeeper, huh? And to be honest with you, honey, I don't think that you using magic to clean up after us is considered housekeeping. More of a magical manager." She said she liked that better anyway. "Good. You may use it anytime you wish. Now, we must pack so that I have time to make love to you before we leave. Might as well break in both houses while we're at it."

"I love that idea, my dear sir. You are brilliant." When she started tossing things in a small bag, he realized that it was one that Raven used. A small bag that would hold just about anything. He wondered if he could get himself one. It was something to look into.

Chapter 5

Butler had enough trouble going on in his life without the townspeople giving him shit. After using a bit of his magic, almost all of it, to rob a bank, it had been about all he could do to get himself home again. While here, he could rest up, get some of his magic back, and try to plan what to do now. The fact that he had the last piece of jewelry was the only thing that kept him going right now. But he had to get things moving in the right direction.

"Did you see the castle?" He was sitting outside the movie theater waiting for a fight to begin when he overheard the kids talking. "My mother said that she has never seen it look so good. And the flowers around it have all the faeries back to work. I was going to go there after school today and see about getting a job. They might have one for you too."

"I already have one. My dad is making sure that the horses are ready for them when they come here. They're coming, you know, all of them. Then we'll have dragons again." The other boy asked his partner if he'd seen any. "No. But my grandma said that at one time, they were as plentiful as the roses in her gardens. And she has a lot of them."

They moved on, and Butler tried to think why the castle was being repaired. He'd not given any orders like that. He didn't have the funds for it even when he wanted to live there. But someone was surely doing it. Wondering if it had been sold for some reason, he limped his way there to see it for himself.

Long ago there had been rumors that the castle hid treasures. He'd been all over the lands and the fallen stones, and nothing. He had wondered if Prisane had hidden it from him with her magic, but knew that couldn't be true. Wherever she was, she was flush, and he wished now he'd beaten her more to get answers. Of course, killing her would have gotten him more money than the scraps he'd been able to gather when she'd been there.

There had been plenty of things for him to sell off, long ago. Her hair brushes had brought him a lot of coin. Everyone wanted a piece of the queen, and he'd really talked it up. But he'd not been able to get another one. She'd hidden them away, along with a lot of other things he'd been meaning to sell off.

He had been able to get to the paintings that had been in the great halls. There was the silver too. Hand forged, and worth a great deal more now than he'd been able to get for it back then. Even with it being the set of silver engraved with her coat of arms, it had only netted him a few coins. Butler laughed too that he'd been able to get to and sell off her teas and cocoas, something that he knew she loved very much.

Her necklace had been the only thing that he'd not been able to part with. And all these years later, he knew that it had to be his one and only good fortune. Marrying Prisane had been easy enough; his father had wanted him to marry, and had paid a dear price for it to happen. Butler had even managed to get ahold of that money and spend it on whores and mead, two of his favorite things.

The trees were much larger than he remembered them to be when he'd been there. When he'd been living in the castle, they'd been mere sticks of wood, tied down so that the winds didn't beat them down. As he made his way up the drive, he noticed that there was new stone on it. The grasses along the side were well kept too. The closer he got to where he remembered the castle to be, the more he worried that someone had bought it when he'd been away, and he'd no longer have access to it.

"Of course when I am king, I'll simply take it back. It was meant for royalty, not some upstart that would live there only but a few times a year, and not care for the things that I will fill it with anyway."

He saw the barn first. It was a large structure and the doors were painted the colors of the flags that had flown over the turrets to the castle. The barn itself was a dark green. If he remembered correctly, that was one of Prisane's colors that she liked to wear.

Moving about, just near the entrance of it, was a man leading a horse around the drive. It was a monster of a thing, its coat gleaming in the sunlight, and its blinders the same color of the barn and livery of the man. Butler wondered how much money was to be had from the people living here, and thought of plans he was going to come up with to get inside before they'd be the wiser. He needed the cash for magic.

The castle came into view then. Butler wouldn't have believed he'd come up the right drive but for the colors on the turrets. The stone that it had been forged from was gleaming with sparks from the stone. There were shutters at the windows too that had never been there before. And the entire front had flowers of every color along not just the castle, but the stone walkway as well. He couldn't believe that this was the same place of so long ago.

"May I help you?" Startled, he nearly fell when a man spoke behind him. Asking him who he was didn't get an answer, but he did tell him that the property wasn't open to the public. "You cannot enter these lands. I'm afraid that you'll need to be on your way."

"I most certainly will not, and I know that it is not for the public, you moron. I own it." The man, guiding yet another horse, this one as white as the snow on yonder mountains, told him that he did not. "Yes, I do. I used to be king of all that you can see. My mate, Prisane, she was the queen before she left me."

"Ah, so you're Butler." Butler was glad that someone remembered him. "We've been warned that you'd be coming around. We're to call the police if you give us any trouble. You're not, are you?"

"Trouble? No, I only want to go into my home and see

what things have been done to it. No one has my permission to do any of this. You're very lucky that I've not called the police on you." The man only smiled at him, and that made Butler angry for some reason. "What is all this going on here? As I've said, I've given no one permission to do all these improvements. And I'm not paying for them either. See if I do."

"It's all been taken care of. You've nothing to worry about. But as for you going into the castle, that's not going to happen. You're not welcome here." Butler asked him why not. "I haven't all the details on it, but I was told that if you were to show up, we're to tell you to be on your way and to leave the buildings here alone."

"I will not." The man simply shrugged and walked by him, the horse flipping his tail so that it hit Butler in the face. "You'll come back here right this minute. You're not to show your back to the king. I said for you to come here until I have given you permission to leave me."

The man kept walking. It was more than he could take, and he moved forward and grabbed the man by the shoulder, thinking to flip him around then dismiss him. But he found himself on his back and the booted foot of the man at his throat.

"I told you not to cause us any trouble or I'd call the police. Now, I'm a man who likes to give a second chance to all, but with you, I think that you'll not learn anything from multiple times no matter the consequences." He wasn't able to move, even when the man lifted his foot. "You be on your way now, and we'll just mark this off as a man who got confused.

Because if you return, I won't be so nice the next time."

"You've not been nice now." He got up, but it took him a few minutes. Butler was heavier than he'd been in his younger days, and even then, he'd been overweight. Plus there was the pain in his belly as well as his arm from when he'd fallen. "I will go into my home, and you'll not stop me."

The man moved, bowing for him to go ahead. Once he was at the sidewalk that was newly put in, he looked up at the walls and wondered if he had remembered it wrong. The stones were larger than he remembered. And he was sure that the place was deeper too, right up and perhaps into the mountain. He'd think of it later. Now he wanted to see his home again.

The doors were wide open. Welcoming, he thought, and was glad that something was going his way for a change. Butler could feel the magic — the place was surrounded by it, and he knew that as soon as he entered, he was going to be fully restored and at his best.

Going to the doorway, he was stopped. There was no one there to keep him from going in. The wall that he could feel wasn't really there. It was magic, and a great deal of it too. Trying to push his way through it only made him weaker, and he stood back to regain his breath. Looking at the two men that had been near the barn, he asked them what was going on.

"You were told not to enter. I told you several times, as a matter of fact. The magic that surrounds all the lands here that go with the castle, they have been enhanced so that you cannot come here to harm it. Or to steal from it." The man he'd been talking to laughed. "I told you, Butler, that we'd been warned about you coming here. Now take yourself away before the police arrive to take you to jail."

"You called them? I didn't take anything as yet. Nor did I get into my home. *My home*, not whoever is living here now. This is where I will live, see if I don't. And the first order of business will be to fire you all." He stomped away when he heard the sirens. "People will rue the day that they made me unwelcome in my own place."

There wasn't any place that he could stay in the town either. Someone, more than likely the same people that had told the men at his home to be on the lookout for him, had told everyone not to do business with him. He would get to the bottom of that too, soon enough.

He had made himself comfortable in an old shed—well, as comfortable as he could, considering that he only had a pillow and a dirty blanket. Lucky for him, he supposed, that it wasn't raining, nor was it cold. Food had been a problem too, until he found himself a field of potatoes and one of corn. It was all he'd eaten since he'd been here, and it was starting to make his belly hurt.

He wandered around for a little more, marveling at the changes to the town. He'd not been here in many a decade, and wondered where all the money was coming from to keep it going. There were new cars along the store fronts, plenty of them. A barber shop, and something about a custom nail place. For the life of him, he couldn't figure out what sort of nails you'd need to be custom. There were even several places to eat—a pizza place and a steak house.

He loved pizza. It was something that he had grown quite fond of over the years. The kind with all the toppings was his favorite, but he liked them with just meat on them as well. He could not stand them with nothing but cheese on them. And he didn't care for people who ate them that way either.

"Well, I don't care for people anyway, so that's not so bad." He laughed at his own joke as he stole away in the cornfield. "If I only had someone to cook this for me, I'd be better off. And some butter too, to rub all along it. I'd be happy as a tick on a dog."

He ate three ears as he picked himself more. Butler felt his belly rumble just as the first cramp hit him. Tearing at his pants, he nearly didn't get them down before he was losing his insides to a bowel movement. Watery liquid seemed to be all there was, but he couldn't stop it from boiling out of him. Twice as he made his way to his home, he had to hide behind a tree or house to empty himself again. He was weak with it by the time he was able to lie down.

Butler was sick, and he knew that someone had poisoned his food. Corn pulled right from the stalk should have been all right, but he knew now that he should have suspected it to be bad. No one left their fields untended like that, without some sort of fence around it. They knew he'd be hungry and made sure that it was there for him to steal. He'd know better the next time.

Moaning the entire night with the pain of his belly, he knew that he'd opened the old wound too. Black ooze seeped from it, and even his wrist was beginning to pain him something terrible. He kept telling himself that he'd be king of the world soon, he just had to go back to the McCades and make them give over their jewelry. Then everything that he ever wanted would be his.

"If I live long enough."

Butler slept fitfully, and when the sun was right in his eyes, he realized that he'd left his door open for things to get in. A cat was sleeping on his head, and he grabbed it and tossed it off him. But it wasn't a cat, but a skunk, and the fucker sprayed its poison all over him before Butler could get away. Crying about his luck, Butler sat there in his own mess, smelling like he'd died, and wondered what he'd done to deserve such a bad time of it.

~~~

Vance hated to fly. It wasn't as bad as some of the cargo planes he'd been on, but he didn't care for the taking off or the landing part. But this time it was made a little easier because Micky held his hand. He just had to remember not to squeeze her quite so tightly when he was nervous. As soon as they landed, he kissed her bruised hand and told her how sorry he was.

"It's fine. See, not even a mark." There wasn't, but he still felt bad for hurting her. "I tell you what. The next time we have to go in a subway for something, you can let me hold your hand. I hate being underground in those things."

"Really? You have a deal. For the record, I love the subway. Not the people in them — like sardines in a can if you ask me — but I do like to ride them." She asked him how many times he'd been able to ride one without people. "You'd be surprised. Sometimes all I have to do is show up dressed out in my gear, and they run off like I'm going to kill them. Makes for a few good laughs for me too."

The family was being met at the hangar as soon as they landed. Looking out the window on his side of the family jet, he could see the three long limos, as well as a cargo van for their luggage. He was glad now that his mom had told him to bring a lot of clothing, as well as his dress clothing. Vance could see that it wasn't like home, but a good deal more formal.

The man that was to meet them was Gerald Pins. He was the person who had been in charge of getting everything ready for them. He spoke to Grady when he found out who he was, and then addressed the rest of them.

"If you'd be so kind as to take a seat in a car, we'll be on our way. The crew here will see to your luggage, as well as anything else you might have brought." The women handed over coats as well, as the day was really warm. "There is a light snack for all of you in the cars that should hold you over until dinner. We have it to be ready at six, if that's all right with you."

Everyone nodded and moved to the cars. He and Lewis with their mates rode in one, the others in the other two. Lewis took several of the little tea cakes, as well as one of the containers of water. Micky asked him if he was always such a pig.

"He is where food is concerned. And don't believe him when he tells you it's for professional reasons either. He's a man that likes food. No matter what it is." Vance laughed at Raven when she told on his brother. Then he took two of the cakes himself, as well as a glass of the tea that was in the little fridge. "Oh my, you need to taste this, Micky. It's so good."

He ate his cakes and the little scone that was offered to him. It wasn't enough to fill him, but it did take the edge off. When he glanced at his watch he thought he could hold out for another hour, but was reminded that there was a four-hour time difference. Vance said he wasn't going to make it for five hours.

"I'm going to need some real food before then. I mean, like a sandwich and some chips or something. There had better be something more than this stuff when we get there." Micky was laughing at him as he bitched about how hungry he was. "I'm seriously hungry. You distracted me this morning, and I didn't get any breakfast."

"I distracted you. You attacked me when I was taking a shower. How is that my fault?" He wiggled his brows at her and Lewis laughed. "He's like this little kid with a new toy around me. Does it ever slow down?"

"No. Not that I'm complaining, but no, it's like that all the time. It's almost as if they are hard twenty-four seven and need someone to take the press off." The women laughed, and Vance felt his face heat up. This wasn't the kind of talk he did around his brothers. "Also, they're hungry more and more the more magic they get. I am too, but as a witch, I am hungrier all the time."

Micky was a faerie, and she needed to have fresh fruits and vegetables. While he could eat them too, they didn't fill him like meat did. Steak was his go to source of protein, and potatoes. But veggies, they filled the void, but didn't last long.

He figured it was his dragon.

"I've not see him yet." Lewis asked him what he meant. "My dragon. I've never—I guess I should have brought him out or something, but I never thought of him. I should probably do that before Butler comes around. I'd hate to have to call him and not have any idea what I'm doing."

"We'll do that after we have a look at the castle and the grounds. I guess the townspeople are having a welcome home party or something for us tonight."

It was a party, but it wasn't for just that. He was getting married tonight, and Raven was going to give him the necklace for the occasion. He looked at Lewis as he continued.

"Mom said that she wanted to go into town tomorrow and do some shopping and such. Are you ladies going?"

"Not on your life." They all laughed at Micky. "Shopping with them once is more than enough for me. I will order online if I need anything, or go by myself. That is just too much, going with them, for one person to be able to handle."

"My lords, the castle is just around the bend here." They rolled down the windows as the driver instructed them to do. And when they stopped at the end of the tree lined drive, Vance got out. "Shall I wait for you, sir?"

"No. I think I'd like to take a walk if you don't mind." The man might have said something, but he didn't hear it if he did. Vance was blown away by the castle that was his family's. Mostly Gabe and Harper's, but they'd said it was for all of them.

"'Tis something else, isn't it?" Vance nodded at the man as he stood beside him. "We had heard that you men were big, but I didn't take it the way that I should have, I'm embarrassed to say. My name is Toby Mannulus. I care for the horses and other barn animals."

"It means pony in Latin." Toby bowed before him and grinned. "I'm Vance McCade. And yes, we are all big men. We have wives too, though they're not at all large, but mean as snakes when pushed. This is beautiful."

"Thank you, my lord. It was in ruin until a few months ago. The first wall going up was our first clue that the magic was coming back. Then as the days went by, the castle started moving to be repaired faster. It's still working on a few things; the building now goes back into the mountain behind it. There are several more bedrooms than there had been before. And lots of improvements that I have come to enjoy." Vance asked him if he'd been here, back then. "In a way, yes. Good of you to know that, sir. But my family was a part of this castle for a great many years before it fell. I'm married to the eldest daughter of Lord Caelin."

"He's a good man. I've only just come to know him." He said that he was the best there was. "And these improvements, I was told that there would be a great deal of security around the place as well. We might have a visitor that isn't welcome here."

"Butler. He's been here. Just this morning, as a matter of fact. We tried to get him to leave by telling him, but he had to try and enter the castle itself. He couldn't, of course, not with the magic in place. And if someone has ill-will in their heart, the thoughts to kill or even to harm anyone within the walls, then that person cannot get in either. It's magic that has kept us all safe in this area for a long time."

Vance liked that. But it might not be enough. Walking around the huge stone building, he could see that there were natural security measures as well. That he knew he could live with.

The walls were two feet thick in most places, more where it butted into the mountain. There were no entrances on the lower level where anyone from the outside could get into the house. But there was a tunnel that would lead the family out, along with staff, when necessary.

"There is a guard on duty at each of the entrances as well. The one in the tunnels is a water buffalo that has also been here for a long time, and the person to the front is a troll. They're not to be messed with even on good days. He comes around in the evening, and is gone when his replacement comes at dawn. He too is a troll, but in a better frame of mind most of the time." Vance told Toby that he'd never seen a troll. "We'll have to rectify that for you then, sir. You might not think you're in for a treat once you meet one. They can be quite foul mouthed when the mood strikes."

Vance was happy, he realized. And relaxed. As Toby introduced him to more of the staff, Vance shook hands with them all and was glad when none of them seemed to like Butler any better than they did. One of the women in the garden—plucking, she told him, not pulling weeds—said that she had helped the queen mother to care for her son when he was but a babe. He liked her very much when she offered to make him a wee bit of a snack.

The *snack* turned out to be a turkey leg, a fried pie, as well as a gallon of lemonade. Vance didn't want to seem like a pig, but with her encouragement, he ate all of it while talking to her. Toby had to see to the stable, so Vance was shown around by Miss April while he finished his meal.

The fruit trees were lined up in neat rows. There were all kinds of fruits too, not just things that he thought would grow there. Miss April told him that the magic of the castle made it, so they could have fruits year-round, and also greenery. He told her his wife was a faerie.

"Yes, we were told that Lady Raven and Lady Micky would be joining you here. The others I haven't met, but I'm sure that they're as sweet as pie." He told her not to bet on that. His mate was a warrior and his mom was considered mouthy. "Oh well, we'll enjoy having them around. No matter the mouth they have."

After he'd made the rounds to as many people as he saw close to the castle, he went inside. He could feel the magic around the place when out of doors. Inside it was thick on him, like he was wearing armor. This was a place he'd feel safe in any day.

Chapter 6

Micky wasn't sure what to think about this. Yes, she did want to marry Vance, but with all these people here as a witnesses, she wondered if anyone had given this a lot of thought.

Like what about Butler coming? What if he tried to hurt them all? And where was the necklace that was supposed to end all this for the family? Butler could have had a fake one there when he killed Raven's mother, just for someone to take from him, and that's what they had now. Also, what if he wasn't nearly as weak as he was letting on? She knew this man and his trickery. He could be just lying in wait and—

"You do know that I can read your mind, right? And while I have thought of all the things that are racing through your mind like a carnival ride, I believe with all my heart I have the right piece." Micky asked Raven how she knew that. "Because, like all the pieces, I can see it for what it is. And you'll see it when it touches you."

"We've not even talked about it. I mean, for me to get it. While I'm not insecure about loving him, maybe he doesn't really care for me. And he doesn't want me to have the necklace at all." Raven popped her in the forehead and laughed. "This isn't the least bit funny. And I can hurt you."

"Maybe you can, but you'd be hurting just as badly. But he loves you. Lewis and I were talking about it last night, how much he's mellowed out. Not so much that he's not out there looking at things to make sure we're safe while we're all here, but he smiles more. Laughter isn't something that he shared a great deal. It's wonderful to see the two of you together. You're both these militant type people, yet when you're side by side, or even just in the same room, it's like you're these mushy people to each other. It might seem sort of gross to some, but to us married ones, we love it."

"He does that to me." Raven nodded. "Vance isn't like you guys see him. He's compassionate, loving, and kind. He cooks, and he loves the outdoors. I mean, I know that I'm different when I'm around him, but I can be myself with him. I don't need to be, nor do I want to be, on guard all the time. I can just lay my head on his shoulder and know that if I happen to fall asleep, he'll make sure that I'm all right when I wake up." Micky flushed, feeling her face heat up. "You must think I'm a sap. I'm not, you know. I can kick anyone's ass and just walk away."

"And for a minute there, I thought you were about to go all mushy on me again." They both laughed then. "I know just what you mean. I'm a witch, and a very powerful one, but with Lewis right next to me, I feel like a pretty woman that has the strongest man in the world right in my corner. But I think we're supposed to feel that way. Secure, yet on guard. Loved and protective at the same time. It's the life we lead that makes us what we are. The good thing is, we all have a balance, a person that is like us but different enough that we mesh well."

After the girl talk, she supposed it was called, she did feel a lot better. Alisha came in to see them a few minutes later, holding a large garment bag and nodding even as she started to shake her head.

"Yes, you'll do this for me. I've been waiting for Vance to get married since he went off to war. And no one has been able to use this dress since my mother helped me get into it when I married his jackass of a father." Micky asked why she should wear it. "It was my mother's. And I told my little boy when he found it hidden in the back of my closet that someday he'd meet a beautiful woman and he could marry her with her wearing it."

"You made that up." Alisha laughed, but told her it really was her mother's. "Then why didn't any of the others wear it? I mean, I'm the last bride, right? Why not Emma? She was first."

"I don't know, honestly. When we were getting ready to come here, it occurred to me that none of the women in this family had ever worn it. It made me sort of sad that I'd never thought about it until then. So, you're the only chance I have for someone from this family to wear my mother's gown." Micky asked her how she knew that it would even fit. "I don't know that either. I'm hopeful, I guess you could say."

It fit. Not only did it fit, but the shoes that had been put into the bag also fit her foot like a slipper. Standing in front of the mirror, Micky looked at herself and couldn't believe it was the same person. Looking over her shoulder, she saw Alisha crying with a pretty blue hankie in her hand.

"I'll need that, I think. Something blue, right? And the dress is borrowed. What else goes with that saying? Let me think. Something old, something new, something borrowed, something blue. I think that's it." Raven corrected her. "Oh, that's right, and a silver sixpence in her shoe. I have no idea where we'd get one of those this late in the game."

"Oh my word."

Alisha dumped her ever present purse out on the table. Micky marveled at the amount of things that she had stashed in that sucker. There was a switchblade that had a pretty pearl handle; a can of mace that lay next to a roll of mints; a half-eaten donut in a plastic baggie that looked as if it had been smashed up against the knife; a tube of lipstick that was taped together; and a brush and several screws, a tiny hammer, and keys. There was also a cell phone that had a cracked front, and a mirror. Micky laughed when she picked up what looked to her like a coin purse that small children took to school a long while ago for their milk money.

"That's what I'm looking for." Alisha opened it up, and there in the middle of her palm was a slightly tarnished sixpence. Taking it from her, Micky looked at her when she saw the date on it. "It's very old. I don't know if that will work double for the old part."

"This *is* very old. It was minted in sixteen-o-one, when it really was made of silver. And you just carry it around with you? In your purse? Aren't you afraid of losing it? Or someone taking it?" Alisha nodded, then shook her head. "I don't understand."

"You've just seen what I carry around. I think some robber would bring me my purse back because he'd feel sorry for me. I'm forever saying I'm going to clean it out, but.... Well, I haven't gotten around to it. But as for the coin, my father gave it to me on the day I married my husband. He told me that Mom had been given it by her mother when she'd married him. Since my mom had passed away when I was younger, he made it his duty to pass it on to me." Micky didn't know what to say. "I didn't mean to make you cry, honey. It's just something that I thought of too."

"You're not a nice person." They all laughed and hugged. Then hugged again. "I don't know what to say. I really don't. You are a wonderful person, a generous and kind woman. No wonder your boys love you so very much."

"I'd very much like for you to love me that much too. All of you." Micky nodded, emotions making it nearly impossible for her to speak. "I've never had so much fun as I have had with you girls. I love my sons, but they didn't understand women, not like they do now. And I can't tell you how happy I am that I'm a grandma, and will someday be a great grandma too. All this, simply because a queen one day decided to use her magic to make it possible for me to have so much love in my heart that I can hardly contain it some days."

"Oh Alisha, you're truly wonderful."

They were a mess by the time they were ready to go out and meet the crowd that had gathered. There were more than there had been when she'd gone out earlier that morning. Micky wanted to turn tail and run, but she saw Vance by the flowers and knew that for him, she would and could do anything.

The minister was there waiting for her when she arrived. Gavin had been kind enough to step in for someone to give her away. He assured her that he was getting good at it, that he'd given away his mom too. Smiling at the cheeky young man, she passed a little magic on to him, knowing that someday he'd need the extra when a woman broke his tender heart. He'd get over it and marry well and happily someday, but in the meantime, he'd be hurt.

Vance kissed her as soon as she got to him. The veil was in his way, so he simply kissed her through it, much to the amusement of his family. When the minister cleared his throat, he told the man that she was just too beautiful not to want to kiss.

"Be that as it may, Lord Vance, there is a way we do things here. Now, dearly beloved, we are here today to see the union of these two people. A dragon and his heart." As he talked about how they were a perfect couple, that they'd live long lives, Micky looked at her mate, her husband to be. And when he squeezed her hands, she realized that she'd zoned out for a moment and had to ask the minister to repeat himself. "I have a feeling that you've not heard a word I've said, young lady."

"Nay, I have not. But I'm older than I look, sir." She winked at him and he laughed. "You were saying?"

"Yes, so I was. Instead of a ring to bless this union, Lord Vance has something different to encircle your love with. If you'd be so kind as to pay attention this time, I've asked you if you're willing to marry this man." She nodded. "You must let everyone know your feelings, my dear."

"YES. YES. YES." Everyone laughed, and she turned to the man again. "Do you think they heard me?"

"I believe those that could not make it today might have heard you. All right then, Lord Vance. You may give her your promise."

She watched as he pulled something from his pocket. The first thing that popped into her head was a gun, and she had to close her eyes to get rid of that image.

"Micky? Are you all right?" She said that she was and looked at him. "I have a ring for you, but not a ring for your finger. I have a ring of magic, a ring of love from a mother to a son. I give to you the McCade necklace, in hopes that it will keep you safe and happy for the rest of our days together."

There was nothing from it, no tingle of magic; nothing to indicate that it was anything more than a beautiful necklace that had been around for a while. Looking around the room, she wanted to pull out her magic, all of it, hunt down Butler, and kill him. Even if they had to start this all over, it—

"Honey?"

Before she could answer him, even if she had one, the magic hit her hard, taking her to the ground and then lifting her up from it again. Vance was with her, his body bowed back from it, his face etched in pain. Looking at the others, she could see that it was taking them the same way. Painfully and quickly.

When she opened her eyes she was lying on the ground. The rest of the wedding party was as well, even Alisha. Sitting up, she looked at the group that had come out to enjoy the day with them, and they erupted into cheers.

Clapping and patting them on the back, they helped everyone stand up. It was the strangest thing she'd ever witnessed, and she went to Vance. Holding him as tightly as he did her, she asked him if he was all right.

"Yes. I feel different, but not sick like I thought I was going to be." He looked at her, and kissed her on the mouth. "We're still not married yet. He has to tell us that part."

"Yes, well, I think we've done all we need to so that we're man and wife." The minister cleared his throat. "You should really see a doctor about that. It could develop into something serious; then where would you be by not being able to marry people?"

"Yes. Later, perhaps, I'll have your future brother-in-law look at it. But for now, how about I do my job while I can. I now pronounce you man and wife. There." Again the crowd cheered. Balloons were let go, birds seemed to come from everywhere, and their whiteness filled the sky. When Vance pulled her into his arms this time, he kissed her with all the passion and love that she felt for him.

"I'd like to officially introduce you all to Lord and Lady Vance McCade. Of the McCade dragons."

Micky was Micky McCade, and as happy as she'd ever been in her life, as happy as she thought she'd never be. And when she was kissed again, all she could think about was that

Butler had better stay his ass away today or he'd be sorry. And dead. She was so over his threats and stupidity.

The feast was delicious. There was a large ham as well as a turkey, and a pig was roasting over a large pit. Side dishes were brought out and set up on long tables, most of them groaning from the weight of it all. Baked potatoes, mashed, and fried. There was winter squash and other vegetables that she knew had come out of gardens she'd seen around the yards. Tea and water were served with wines and beer. It was the best food and the greatest company that she'd ever been with. And Vance never left her side.

Music was playing under one of the large trees on the castle grounds. She danced with all the brothers, and they in turn danced with their mom. Pictures were taken of all of them, and some of just the two of them. Alisha had her join her and Vance when the photographer wanted one of the son and mom. There were pictures of everyone that was there, and of all the food as well. When they were posing for pictures for themselves, a nice gentleman came to her and handed her a rose of Sharon, one of the flowers that she had always loved. Micky pinned it to her dress and danced with him.

~~~

"How you feeling?" Vance asked Grady what he meant. "Well, you should be able to shift now. And with that piece that you put on Micky, we should all have this armor. But I don't feel any different. With each piece, I've felt a little of it, but nothing from this. I was wondering how you felt. Maybe, like the knowledge, it has to take a minute or two."

"I feel like I'm encased in it. You think that's all it is?

Because I have to tell you something, I don't feel the dragon anymore. I was afraid when I first realized it, but it might just be what you said, because I have to wait." Grady said he didn't know. "Yeah, me either. We're sure that this is the right piece, right? I mean, it's not a fake and we're all going to be fucked when Butler gets here."

"No, I'm sure that it's the last piece. But what I don't understand is your dragon. I felt mine even before Harper got here. Does Warrior speak to you?" Vance told him that he'd never heard from him. "I don't know then. I'm sort of worried."

"I am too, now." Grady said he was sorry to have brought it up. "No, don't be. I was concerned anyway. This isn't anything new with our lives right now. I mean, it seems like every day is something else going ass up. What if Butler comes here and we're not ready? Or we can't call the dragon? Christ, I have more questions than I did before. But I don't want to worry anyone just yet. It might be that it's our wedding and the magic somehow knows that."

"Could be." But Grady didn't sound any more certain than he did. "How do you like this place? I mean, I expected nothing to be here other than some fallen stones and a few overgrown trees that would need to be removed. This is...this is magnificent. And the beds, we slept like a rock last night. You?"

"Yes. I was afraid we'd be up all night worrying about one thing or another. But almost as soon as my head hit the pillow, I was out like a light." Grady talked about the castle and they discussed the way things were around the property.

The fields where corn and other grain was grown were ready to be planted. The fruit trees were in full bloom. He'd even seen a few fruits that he had no idea would grow here. He supposed, like his brother, it was the magic. "You have a stable here. And from what I heard, they're all trained to be around other shifters. So, you could just ride them right away."

"I've never been on a horse." They were teasing each other about that, and how much weight one could handle, when his brothers joined them. It was really nice to have them all around all the time now. And if he needed a break from it, just being around people, he could simply walk away and they seemed to understand. Looking around the yard, he saw that Micky was sitting with some of the other women from the village, as well as his mom. Whatever they were talking about, they seemed to be having a good time.

Vance thought about trying to contact the dragon, or Caelin and his mom. But he was a little nervous about it. Not about talking to them, but about not being able to. What if he'd been wrong about his dragon? Maybe he'd never had one at all, and this would have to begin again. When Kenton snapped his fingers in front of his face, he noticed that the others had walked away while he'd been worrying himself sick over this.

"I don't have a dragon." Kenton said that he did. "I don't think so. I haven't heard from him. Nor has Warrior spoken to me. What if there isn't one in my body, and all this has been for nothing?"

"Calm down. Have you tried to contact your dragon, or anyone else?" He shook his head. "Well, I think that it worked.

I mean, the rest of us felt something when it touched her skin. Have you tried touching your skin to where the necklace is?"

"No. Is that what you had to do?" He told him that Emma had touched the ring to his heart and he could shift. "I've not done that. I never thought about that part."

Vance looked for Micky, wanting to try it right now. But Kenton grabbed his shoulder to stop him from advancing toward her. He asked him if he was calm yet.

"Calm? No, not in the least. Why? What happens if I'm not calm?" Kenton told him. "Yeah, I can see scaring a lot of our guests with this. I've never been so scared in all my life. Not even when I've been in front of a firing squad."

"You've been in front of a firing...? You know what, I don't want to know. Yes, you'll scare everyone here if you go off halfcocked like you are." No one had ever called him that before. He was always calm and knew just what he was going to do and how to make it happen. But right now, he felt like his head was going to explode, and he didn't care for that feeling. "Just calm yourself and I'll let you go. You're starting to draw attention to yourself, and you don't need that either. If we looked worried, like you do right now, then everyone is going to be worried, and that would be bad. So just take some breaths in and out and then you'll be all right. I hope."

"No. No, I don't want to start a mass hysteria. I'm better now, but not great." He looked at Kenton and smiled. "I'm wondering how you call to the dragon."

"I don't know. If you mean Warrior, he never shuts up. Which is what has surprised me with you. But if you mean your dragon, because you do have one, then all I do is think

94

about him and I can shift. Just try that first."

Closing his eyes, he thought of a dragon—his, he supposed. But there was nothing there. The sword was there, shining like a new penny in the ground, but nothing to do with a dragon. Then he reached for Warrior, just saying his name as if they'd been friends forever.

"Warrior, are you there?" He said that he was. Vance felt his knees buckle, and had Kenton not caught him, he would surely have hit the ground. But he did go all the way down, just so he'd not fall a second time. Calmly, he spoke to the dragon. "I was wondering about my dragon."

Your dragon, my lord? You have no dragon. Vance told Kenton what he'd said. *You have no use for the dragon, sir. You have the sword.*

"Am I to change into a sword?" Warrior said that he didn't think so, but he would search for information for him. "Have I ever had a dragon?"

Yes, when you were born, you all had them. But since you have had the sword come to you, you no longer have it. There is, from what I can remember, no need for you to have it. I'm not entirely sure why, but I will look, as I have said. He nodded and sat there waiting. *It might take me some time to find it, my lord. I have only just gotten all the information that I've had before I was only a spark. Give me some time, then I will have it for you.*

"I don't have a lot of time, Warrior. I mean, Butler could be here at any moment. And if he comes and we're not ready, I don't know what will happen to you." He said he wasn't worried. "No, you'd not be, I guess, but I just got married today. And while I won't die, nor will the rest of us, I'd really

95

rather not spend it all banged up because I don't have a dragon."

The riches, they are for all of you. Vance said he wasn't worried about any money. *There are more than just monetary gains, my lord. Much more than that. I can remember a lot more, and I do remember taking a great many treasures to be hidden away for you and your family. That, too, might take me some time to find. I'm like a newly born dragon. I'm learning as I go.*

"So long as I have Micky as my wife, then I couldn't care less if we lived in a cardboard box. I love her that much." Warrior told him he didn't understand. "That's fine. You go ahead and see what you can find out, and I'll wait for you. But if he comes here, I'm not sure what we're to do about this."

He will not be there today, my lord. He is recovering. The magic that came when you put the necklace on your other half, he was harmed with it as well. It took a great deal out of him, and from what I understand, he didn't have much anyway. Vance liked the idea of him being weaker, and told Kenton what he'd found out. *There is much information, but none of it is clear. Your family is the first generation to have ever completed this. And you are the first one to have gotten the Sword of Caelin.*

"Fat lot of good it'll do me if I can't pull my dragon to help." Warrior said that he would do some research. Vance looked at Micky while talking to his brother. "I don't know what I'm supposed to do now. Not just with this dragon stuff, but at all. I'm out of work as of the middle of next month. I'm on a sabbatical until I get out of the service."

"You can do pretty much anything you want, Vance. You could do nothing and still be able to live nicely. You could work for yourself. Open some kind of private investigation office and do that. Though, I don't know if I'd recommend that. You might beat the shit out of the person you're supposed to be following around." Vance laughed. "You'll be just fine. You won't have to live in a box, and if you do, Micky can come and live with us."

"Gee, thanks." They laughed again. "I'll be all right. I just, after being on my own for a while, making decisions about my own life, it's difficult to think that I'm responsible for another person. Who could, I think, take care of both of us without breaking a sweat."

"Same here with Emma. I love her to death, but there are times when her mind goes all villain, and I worry about what she's going to teach our children." Vance had always loved her for the way her mind worked, and told Kenton that. "Yes, well, you should watch television with her, especially crime movies or shows. She can pick it apart faster than I bet Dalton can. Not to mention, she has it all figured out within the first five minutes. I don't even watch them with her anymore."

"Yes, you do. And you love it. And her." He said that he did, then asked Vance if he was all right. "Yes. I suppose. I'm still clueless, but I do feel better now that I've let some of it go. Thank you for helping me stay sane."

"You're very welcome. You can do the same for me when our child is born. That way, when I freak the fuck out, because I've no doubt that I will, you can hold my hand." He said he might be more inclined to hurt him. "You do, and Emma will hurt you back. She's my hero."

Vance got up from the ground and walked to where

Micky was. She looked so beautiful in Mom's gown. The guests talked about the castle with him and her, telling them how it had come up over a period of time, but in the last few weeks, much faster. Vance was glad something was going right.

The gifts that were given to them had been a surprise. There were mounds of them on a table, and a lot of envelopes in a large basket at the end of the decorated table. Vance hadn't been to a wedding in a long time, so had to ask his mom if they opened them there or they waited until they were home.

"Here would be nice. Since we don't know these people, when their gift is opened, they can come to you two and you can acknowledge them personally. I think that would be a lovely thing to do." He wasn't so sure about that. He wasn't much of a people person, and neither was Micky. "You're going to be just fine, Vance. Trust me."

In the end they opened about half of them there and took the envelopes to their room. There were just too many people to talk to, and the ones that they did all had a story to tell them about the gift. Vance hated that they'd run out of daylight. He was enjoying each and every one of them, as well as the stories that they told.

Chapter 7

Butler lay as still as he could. He was sure that the earth was going to open up and swallow the whole town soon. When the ground had shaken, he had been as terrified as he'd ever been.

He'd not seen anyone all day, and he wondered if there had been a big announcement that said to get out of town and he'd not heard about it. Getting up slowly, careful where he stepped, he went out of his little shack and into the darkening evening.

The sun had fully been up when he'd felt the earth move. He might have known more about what was going on, but he'd fallen over, and then a large piece of the boards that held his roof up fell down over him and hit him on the head. It didn't help that he was nearly as weak as a kitten and his belly was seeping again. Nothing was going right for him.

He'd heard in town that the McCades were here. He'd

not expected them to come here at all, much less before they got all the pieces. He was glad for it, really. It would save him the time and expense of going to find them. Getting here had been the hardest trip he'd made. No magic to speak of, no funds, not even a copper penny, and food was almost as hard to find as magic.

These people were going to be easy pickings because of their stupidity, and he was going to make them suffer when this was all done. But the town was all a twitter about them being here, and he couldn't help but be envious of how they were being talked about. Like they were kings of the land and he was nothing more than a pauper down on his luck. Perhaps, he thought, that was the reason they were here, to see if the last piece was here. It was, but not in a way that they'd ever lay their hands on it.

"It is. If they cared to get close enough for me to kill them then I could take what they have and be rich beyond my wildest dreams. Then we'll see how the townspeople bow down before me. Just before I remove their heads." Which was saying a great deal; Butler had some pretty wild dreams about money. He laughed at his own funny and held his head. "Damn hovel. Once I'm in the castle, I'm going to rest for a month of Sundays."

The shops were all closed up, and even the benches that some of them put their wares on had been put inside. He wondered if that was to keep him out, but he had no way of knowing since they all seemed to be gone. Even the houses that usually had a curl of smoke coming from the back yard for a grill out were silent as a tomb. He wondered about that when something else had occurred to him. There were no cars to be seen anywhere. They were usually lined up and down the street like stones on a walkway.

"Mayhap they're all dead." He wasn't sure if that was a good thing or not, but then he realized that dead men didn't lock their doors and bring in the products they were hawking. "Nay, just gone for the day. And not even an invite for me to join them."

Every day he met someone else that was hostile toward him. Butler was amazed that they could hold a grudge for so long. He'd done this or that to their family. Or he'd stolen something in the last few days from them. He was not even given the chance to defend himself or his actions. The thing that really stuck in his craw was the fact that they hated him so much for whatever he'd done to their aunts, cousins, or whoever. Like he should be punished for trying to make himself a son that would be just like him. Pussies, that's all they were. And he'd never had to resort to rape, as they accused him of. He was a man that was king, and everyone knew that a king had special privileges.

Butler would show them all when he was king again, and then they'd have to treat him better. He was going to tax them too, until they had nothing left and he had it all. After he took all their women to his bed and planted a child in every one of their bellies. It would be the first rule he made them adhere to. He was fucking king, after all.

"Stupid people."

Taking a walk because he needed to keep moving in order to keep his bones from stiffening up, Butler thought of the McCades. He wondered what they'd say if he just headed to the hotel and tried to talk to them. Not that there were that many hotels around, but he wasn't even sure where to begin with his search. Butler had to sit down only after a few yards — he'd never been so weak before.

Butler knew that he was going to need to find himself some magic soon. Right now he wasn't sure that he could take on a small child, much less the McCades. The only thing going in his favor at this point was that they were just too stupid. And he knew they were because of how they were going about things. He would have done things differently had he had money like they seemed to have.

For instance, he would have dressed in the finest clothing. Silks and velvets that were so purple that they looked black. And he'd have his own crest designed too. He had never liked the one that had been on the castle door. It had been dragons, and there weren't going to be any around when he was finished. Also, he'd have a feast every night with singing and dancing, and naked women for him to take when he wanted. Christ, all they seemed to do was work, work, work. Like there wasn't anything else to occupy their time.

It hadn't escaped his notice that the McCades all lived in fine houses, drove nice trucks, and didn't seem to have a care in the world. Had he been them, he would have gotten the pieces as they had, but then killed off the women so they'd not be such a bother. And they were, too. Every woman had her place, and the McCade women hadn't seemed to be put into theirs yet. Standing, he started limping to get moving again.

102

These women of the McCades went about like they were ruling the roost. They had their own money too, it seemed to him, and spent it on things that were only for themselves — he'd seen the boxes at their trash cans. And they didn't cook. Not a one of them seemed to be at home making a meal for their mates, but had other people doing it. And the house where someone did cook, he did it for his wife. Like that was something special.

As he made his way to the orchard where he'd gotten a couple of apples yesterday, he saw a long line of cars down the road that led to the castle. He wasn't sure what was going on, but he decided to have him a looksee. Maybe it was a funeral, he hoped, and all the McCades had been killed for him.

Everyone there was dressed in their finery. There was a nice smell of food that made his belly growl a little too. But as hard as he tried to get close enough to see what was going on, he couldn't get any closer.

There was a large tent in the front of the castle; he could just barely make out the poles that held it up and the colors of Prisane's own crest at the top. Butler could see long tables of what he thought was food, but couldn't be sure. Then there were the gifts. They were closer to him, and he could see the ridiculous ribbons on the boxes. A waste of money, as far as he was concerned.

"It all comes in a box or a bag anyway. Why waste the time and money to pretty things up that are not going to mean a hill of beans once they tear into it? And who could be having such a grand affair that I'd not heard about it? I've been about the town all week, and nothing was said." He was nearly to the table of the gifts when he realized that they weren't gifts at all, but empty boxes and torn papers. "Can't even have a proper party. Whoever these fools are, they're going to know what it's like to see someone having a good time when I'm in charge."

The orchard seemed less like a place that he wanted to get his meal from now. The food that he could smell, a roasting pig, was the most wonderful smell he'd ever encountered, and it seemed a great let down for him to have just an apple or so. Instead, he went back to his little place and sat on the rags he had for a bed.

"I have to get me something to use. Magic. You'd think in a place like this, there'd be something." He had been in the fields in the early morning, looking for a faerie or two. Even the brownies, who were dumber than rocks, seemed to have gone into hiding. "I could go to the mountain, I suppose. Look there."

But the thought of going there, climbing the mountain even for magic, seemed a task that was too much for him. He was exhausted most of the time, and he could barely move around the rest. Being without his magic was like having his teeth pulled out and a steak, a fine rare one, set before him.

Butler would have to do something, and the sooner the better. He needed those pieces they had, and he wasn't going to get them without more magic than he had on him now. He'd forgotten how much he had come to depend on the magic and all that it had done for him. Like his body falling apart. His teeth, never in good shape in the first place, were hurting him all the time now.

Butler was even beginning to look older. There wasn't enough to keep him alive, much less make him look like a young man who had had it all. He would again, soon too, but for now, he was living in a shack without heat or water, and he was hungry. All the time.

Resting for a little bit, he thought about the necklace and how it was supposed to be this all-powerful thing. He had, at one time, been able to rub the blue diamond in the middle and replenish himself for several days. Now all it gave him was a shiny stone and a sore thumb.

After napping for a few hours, he made himself walk to the mountain. Stopping by the orchard this time, he picked himself several apples, a few pears, and a fruit that looked like it had scabs all over it, with the ugliest hard stems out of the top of it. It was the most dreadful thing he'd ever seen, but he figured that as big as it was, he should be able to get some energy from it. The walk was made more difficult with his extra weight, and he thought about just sitting down again and resting.

"Can't do it." Butler had been talking to himself for all his life, and thought that he needed to pep himself up more instead of thinking of only bad things. Like how hurt he was, and how hungry he seemed to be all the time. "Can't rest until this is done. I will win this. I will."

Butler felt better for it each time he said it. Of course he had to stop and rest when he talked; he didn't seem to have enough breath to walk and talk at the same time. Way up in the mountain, it was colder too. So that didn't help his health nor his disposition one single drop.

The trek nearly killed him, but it was nearly sunrise when he finally got to an area where there were flowers still growing. He didn't remember there being so many tangles on the ground when he'd come this way hunting for a woman to warm his bed. Not only were the trees overgrown with scrub brush under them, but brambles just reached out and scratched at his face. Even his bag of fruit had been battered and he'd lost almost all of it; the ugly thing had been the only item that remained in the bag — Butler thought it was because of the spikes at the top and it getting all tangled up in the plastic. It had better be worth it, he thought to himself.

He saw her a full minute before it registered that she was what he was looking for. The faerie, all shiny and flittering around the last of the blossoms around the flowers, was singing a tune that made him want to scream at her to shut up. Butler hated music of any kind, and especially hated singing. But for now he'd tolerate it, just to get up close enough to her that he could snatch her up.

Being as quiet as he could, he moved toward her, careful now to keep his eyes on anything else that might be with her. Faeries had a thing for keeping bears and the like with them when they were about. It was just so they'd not be caught in a snare or anything else that would trap them. Butler could not believe his luck as he reached out and grabbed her.

"You're going to help me." She shook her head and he nodded at her. "You are. Or I'll pluck your wings off you and leave you on the ground to be eaten by bugs. You don't want that to happen, do you?"

"You'll do it anyway, Butler the Traitor." He loved the

106

title, and wondered where it had come from. But he'd not allow her to know that. Then they'd stop calling him such a mean sounding name. "What do you think I will do for you? Give you my magic? You may have it—I've not much of it."

"You'll give it to me anyway. And you're going to call all the faeries here to you. I will use you all to get what is mine." She told him she was alone. "No faerie is ever alone. I know that from when I was king here. You'll call them to you and tell them to hurry. I have things to do, and you're going to help me."

She kept telling him she was alone. And no one else came when he made her scream by plucking her wing off. He didn't want her to die, not until he was finished with her, but he was disappointed that she had no others around to feed his magic. Well, if she wouldn't help him the way he wanted, he'd just have to kill her and take it all. He kind of liked that idea better anyway.

Holding her above his head by both hands, he said the words that would give him her all. Her screams were giving him a worse headache, but this was just what he wanted and needed. As soon as he tore her body in half, he felt her magic rain down over him.

It was heady to have so much after being deprived of magic for so long. The first thing that he wanted to do was make himself look better. Give himself a home, new clothing, and a fine feast. But he did none of those things. Not that he thought that what she'd given him would do all that; Butler was sure she'd held out on him toward the end anyway. But he needed to conserve his magic, so that when the time came for him to make the McCades pay, he'd be able to do it.

Butler found four more faeries while he was out. He could not believe his luck today, and was glad now that he'd made the trip. Even though it had cost him a great deal of energy and pain to get here, it was more than he'd hoped for in the way of magic. He'd have enough now, if he was very careful, to take down the McCades.

"I don't need to kill them all. Just one of them and the rest will give me what I want. It's not like they can make it work anyway. Not with me having the final piece." He laughed as he sat in the forest that had been so good to him. "I'll confront them on the morrow, and then by evening I'll have all the magic I need to take back my homeland and rule the world. The dragon and all the riches will be mine to have."

He was near giddy with the prospect of living in the newly remodeled castle. It would surely have all the comforts that he'd grown to love in the last years. Heat and cooling when necessary. A soft bed that would be big enough for him to not just sleep in, but to enjoy some fun with a few whores. They were all whores to him, women of the world, and he'd take his fill of them whenever he wished. Also, he'd hire himself a cook. One that could bake as well as the woman in the town where the McCades lived. He'd have himself pies and cakes whenever the mood struck him. Yes, Butler thought, I'm going to finally have what is coming to me.

Trying to eat the ugly fruit had made him sick. And it had hurt his teeth. Biting into the thing like an apple had been bitter and rough. He had cuts on his lips and tongue, and his chin, where the juice had run over the open sores, was burning like he'd been set on fire. Not having any idea where the thing had come from originally, he decided that he'd be better served to have the plants cut down and be done with them. The plant was good for neither man nor beast, and he thought it very obnoxious too.

Making a mental note to have only apples and oranges in his orchard, the only things that he had recognized while there, he would have them for every meal. Either in a pie or in wine, Butler thought with a laugh.

Walking back to the town in the darkness, he noticed that while there were people walking about, the store fronts were still not opened. It was kind of late, he supposed, but they should have at least opened for a couple of hours. How was he to steal him something good if they didn't cooperate with his schedule? He was beginning to think that the castle had become not a residence as he'd first assumed, but a party house for the town. There was no one person who could afford such a grand place, and they used it for get togethers. That would soon stop too.

He slept in his shed but knew that this time tomorrow he'd be in his own home with his own things. It would have been easy for him to make himself a nice place for the one night, but he didn't want to use his energy. Butler thought that was the first time in his life that he'd thought that. Magic had always been something that was plentiful for him, and easy to get when he needed it. As it was, he was lucky to have what he did, and didn't want to use it needlessly. He would when he had it all, of course. There would be an endless supply of it, he knew it. And if there wasn't, he'd order it to be so. Butler was never going to be without his magic ever again.

"Tomorrow, when I rise, I'll find them at the hotel and finish this once and for all. I'm done with them and their ways." Laughing, he rolled to his side and fell asleep. The walk had worn him out.

~~~

Vance watched Micky sleep. They'd made love all night long and well into the morning, and he knew that she was exhausted. He was as well, but he had a great deal on his mind and he just couldn't shake the feeling that he was going to be the one that messed things up for his family.

"You're thinking too loudly." Micky turned and looked at him, and he smiled with her. "I can almost taste how hard you're thinking about things. What is it? You had something happen or someone said something to you at the party. What was it? And who am I going to have to murder for upsetting you?"

"No one. I promise." He kissed her when she rolled over and on top of him. "I think you don't really want to know. Otherwise, you'd not be naked on me and me as hard as a rock."

"First of all, you're always hard as a rock. It's a wonder you can even think with all the blood in your groin. Secondly, I do want to know, but maybe we can talk later, after I've had my way with you."

Vance helped her sit up. She could ride him anytime she wanted, and he'd not mind at all. But when she only sat over him, just staring down at his face, he asked her what was wrong. When she shook her head, he got worried.

110

"Have I grown a second head and don't know it? Tell me. You're seeing something there. I have food in my teeth?" She laughed, and his worry went down a great deal. "Tell me, love, and then I'll tell you what I've been thinking about."

"You're different. I don't know how yet, but there is something about you that I can't quite put my finger on." He then told her about his thoughts about his dragon. "You don't think he's there with you? Have you ever felt him?"

"No. I mean, yes. I've known that there was something within me that made me think it was the dragon, but now that I'm supposed to be able to call to it, I can't." She asked if he'd talked to his brothers. "Yes. I can speak to Warrior, which I wasn't able to do before you came into my life. He said that he doesn't know either, but that I don't have a dragon now. But I was born with one."

"That doesn't make sense. If you don't have a dragon, how are you guys supposed to call him forth? Not to mention, how do you deal with Butler? He's coming, and I'm betting that he won't exclude you simply because you don't have one." Vance told her that's all he'd been able to think about. "I'm sorry. I wish you had told me. All I could think about was that you'd come to realize that I'm not for you."

"Never that." He took her to the bed, rolling her to her back as he settled over her. "It matters little to me if I ever have a dragon or not, so long as you're beside me."

"I love you as well. But I do worry about you." He told her he was sorry. "No need for that. Just tell me when something is bothering you. I don't want to have to rape your mind when you could just as easily let me know."

111

"You can rape other parts of me if you want." He slid into her, feeling her heat and tightness wrap around him. "I don't think I'll ever get enough of you, how you make me feel. And what you make me want."

"A child." He lifted his head a little, not sure that he'd heard her right. "I want to have your child. Carry a baby that we both created. I know that this thing with Butler is going to end soon, and that we'll come out of it victorious. But right now, all I can think about is having your baby and raising him or her to be person just like their daddy."

"I love you so very much, Micky." He made love to her then. Touching her skin, feeling her respond to him. Never once did he look at anything but her eyes, wanting to see every emotion that she was having.

"You're going to make me come." He grinned and told her he hoped so. "Come with me, Vance. Come with me and let me have your child."

"I don't know how this works with you." Micky told him he was doing a very good job of it. "No, I mean, are you in heat? Do you have a time when you can have a child? I don't know anything about your kind."

"Come in me and we'll have a child. I'm fertile when I want a child with my mate." She cried out and he had to come, come with her. When she said his name, he came hard, filling her body with his seed. "Again. I need you again."

This time he moved down her body to the very heat of her. She was wet, both from him and her need. Licking her from gate to clit, he tasted everything and needed more. Burying his mouth over her, Vance ate her like a feast, devoured her like he was never going to have a meal again.

Micky played with her breasts, tugging at her nipples as he watched her from his position between her thighs. She rolled her hips up to meet his mouth, lowered them when she'd had too much. Lifting her up, cupping her ass in his hands, he felt his cock fill tightly as she came three times in quick climaxes. He wanted to feel her again, taste her mouth, her breasts while he fucked her.

Vance moved up her body this time, tasting her delicious skin, licking her navel and tasting her there. Her ribs were like a fine steak. The underside of her breasts tasted of warm rolls, the yeast at their peak for him to eat. Every part of her was something that he enjoyed. Her nipples were suckled. The lobes of her ears were delightful to nibble on. When he touched his mouth to hers, all he could think about was she was his, all of her, and she wanted to have their child.

Fucking her now, hard and quickly, he thought of her large with their baby. The way it would suckle at her breasts. Watching her when she played with him or her in their yard. It mattered little to him the sex of the child. He wanted healthy and happy, and he knew that together, they could do that.

When he came this time, filling her with his love in addition to his seed, Vance knew that they'd done just what they had wanted. A child would come to them, and it would be a boy. Vance hadn't any idea why he knew that, but he did. And he would be called Caelin Vance McCade.

When he woke up, not even realizing that he'd dozed off, he was alone in the bed. There was a note beside him on the pillow, and he read it while making his way to the bathroom to shower. Micky had gone into town with his sisters and would be back at dinner. Showering and then dressing, he asked her if she was having fun.

I am. Did you get some rest? Vance told her that he felt wonderful. *I'm so glad. So do I, as a matter of fact. And had your mom not called me and asked me to go with them, I might have slept until you did.*

You should have woken me. She said that he was sleeping so well, she didn't want to. *I feel like I'm rested. Things have been disturbing my sleep a little more than I thought they had. But I can honestly say, I don't think I even dreamed last night. You wore me out. Anytime you want to make me sleep like that again, you don't let anything stop you.*

I won't. But you promise me that you'll talk to me next time and not hold it in. I know you probably did that a lot before, but not anymore. I don't want to have to worry that you're keeping something from me when I can help you too. All right? He told her that he loved her. *And I love you too. I hope it's all right, but I've been having so much fun picking out baby things. I've not said anything to anyone yet, but I'm making us a list. You and I, we'll go shopping after we tell everyone that we're expecting. I think that should be something we do.*

You get whatever you want. We have the jet, and if that isn't big enough, we'll come back for it. I love it here. It's all so fresh and clean. And I feel like I've come home. He smiled as he pulled on his socks. *Not enough to live here all the time, I don't think, but I'd very much like to come back here often. If Grady wouldn't mind.*

Are you kidding? They're making plans for Thanksgiving and Christmas this year for coming here. Also, I think there was

114

a mention for Valentine's Day, New Years, as well as all our birthdays. We'll be here a lot between now and when our child is born. He thought about telling her that it was a boy, but didn't have an explanation as to why he thought that. *I'll be home by dinner. We're grilling out, I guess.*

Vance found his brothers in the big living room. They were watching a football game on the biggest television he'd ever seen. When he joined them there, he was given a tall glass of tea and told there were snacks on the buffet. As he made his way there, he laughed.

"Snacks? This looks like a full meal here. Who ordered all this?" Grady said the cook had brought it all in and said for them to taste it. "And what, they'll make it for us again? That sounds like we're all going to need to have a gym membership if we stayed here very long."

"So far, none of us have found anything that we didn't want more of. And there are some things that I've wanted to horde for myself." He joined him at the long table of hot and cold food. "There are drinks too. However, I've not had to get up to get more since I was given my first glass. Someone comes around and refills them about the time they're empty. It's the best football party I've ever been to."

"You think they're glad to be cooking for someone again? Did you try those puffy potato things? I don't know what's in them, but they're delicious." Grady didn't either but loved them too. Grady also pointed out the chicken wings that looked like turkey legs, as well as the buffalo dip and chips.

Sitting down with his family, Vance had two plates of food. When Lewis tried to take some of it, he told him to get his own. The rest of them made a trip to the buffet then, and came back with enough food for them to share with him as well. Vance could get used to this, having a good time with his brothers and fantastic food to eat.

Halftime brought them more food, this time desserts. He was not going to be able to eat dinner at this rate, and tried to pace himself. And as soon as he heard what they were going to have, grilled steaks and shrimp with pasta, he decided that he'd had enough for now. But he did ask the maid that was in the room with them keeping the plates cleaned up if she'd put him back some of the cherry pie, his favorite.

"The cook is making several for dinner tonight, my lord." He thanked her and was ready to tell her to just call him Vance when she spoke again. "Butler will be here on the morrow. I was to tell you when we heard."

Then she was gone, like she'd only been in the room for that one purpose. Putting his plate down, he went back to the couch and sat down. Everything was soured now. He was too nervous again that he'd let his family down when Butler got there. There was still no word from Warrior, and he was beginning to think he was afraid to come back and tell him he had fucked up somehow.

The women showed up just as the game was ending. Vance tried his best to pay attention to the things going on around him, but he couldn't. Instead of trying, he simply gave up and told them all what was wrong with him. And that Warrior was looking to see why he no longer had his dragon and something about the sword was the reason, but he was so despondent that he knew they would hate him. They were screwed, and he knew it was going to be his fault.

"You worry too much. We've made it this far." He nodded at Dalton, who had always been the one, to him, who had the most level thoughts. "The set is with us. We have our mates and children on the way. The magic is here for us to use, and we're going to finish this thing with Butler once and for all. I have to believe that because to even think of the alternative is depressing. We're going to do this, Vance, all of us. And when we do, you'll see that your lack of a dragon was what made it happen."

Vance started to say that he didn't know how that was going to work when Lewis stopped him from talking. "We're a family. All of us have a part to play in this. Not just us, but the women that we love too. Like Dalton said, we'll get through it, and we'll be better men for it. As someone said before, no one has ever made it this far, so there are bound to be glitches. We'll do this."

"And if we don't? What are we out? Nothing." Vance nearly disagreed with Jorden, but didn't. If they didn't make this work, they would all die because the magic for them would be gone; Butler would make sure of that, Vance was positive, but he could see his brother's point too. "We're not out anything that we didn't have before, yet we have gained so much. We're just fine. And we'll win. I know it."

He certainly hoped so. And when they went into dinner a little while later, he did feel better. Still no word on his dragon, but he did have a lot more than he did before. Including a baby on the way.

Chapter 8

Caelin mourned the death of each of the faeries they found. He loved all the creatures of the forest, but the faeries were his favorite. He looked at his son when he asked him if he wanted him to carry them to the faerie circle with him, and Caelin told him he'd do it. He supposed his son was trying to save him the grief, but it was too profound.

"I'm sorry, Father. I thought that they'd been warned to stay out of the forest for now." Caelin said that he had warned them, but some of them had thought they were safe to work. "Those poor creatures. I hate that they gave their life to that man."

Caelin had never told his children anything different than what he knew of his father. They all knew that the man was their grandfather, but they never thought of him like that. He was always that man, or the monster. He supposed that had things gone differently they might have called him grandfather, but that was old news, and nothing could be done about it now. Although secretly, Caelin thought that his father would have hated being called that as well.

Putting the last of the dead into their little burial shrouds, he said a quick apology to Lady Earth and told her that he'd take care of them. The burial shroud was nothing more than a large leaf that was wrapped around them and tied with a piece of reed. Everything would go back to the earth, and sometime in the future flowers of the most beautiful colors would spring up over them. Some of the very plants they'd been working on had been born the same way.

He and his son worked through most of the morning making things right for the forest. Caelin could talk to all the things in here, including the trees and plants. Asking about the man who had killed the poor things had been his first query, and now he talked to them about having someone contact him when he returned. Mighty Oak said that he didn't think he'd come back.

"Why? Do you think he got all that he wanted? Are we to find more of our creatures about?" Mighty said no, that they were all found, but he had been very taxed when he'd gotten here and left. "So, he won't return because he is lazy. I can see that with him. He has always been the sort of man who would take before he tried to get for himself. And take he did, of everyone and every living thing in the world. I am most sorry about all this. I hope that one day soon, we'll no longer have any problems with him."

He is most dangerous, my lord, but he was thinking that he had enough magic to contact your family, the newly arrived ones.

Caelin told him how they were going to bring Warrior out. *Yes, we have heard, and we are all very excited for the magic to return. You must be as well, to have things put to rest after so long.*

"I am. Very much so. And the castle is finished too. Have you heard?" Mighty said that he had. "When we are finished here, I shall have someone come and clean around your roots. I hadn't been here in a long time, and it has gotten too dense for you and the other trees."

Thank you, my lord. I only hope that the new residents at the castle are as kind as you are. He said that they would be. *That's wonderful to hear. We all hope, you know, but we're afraid to believe. It has been so long in coming, but this is good news. Very good news, sir.*

He and his son worked on some of the denser areas until lunch time. Caelin came across the fruit and the pineapple that had been bitten into. He and his son laughed for a good twenty minutes with that. What sort of fool bites into a pineapple without peeling it first? Shaking his head, Caelin planted the remnants of it and then set off for home. It was time to ready things for his family dinner tomorrow. It would be the beginning of the end for them all.

After lunch, he made his way to the castle. There were things that he needed to talk to them about. Some of the houses that they now owned, as well as buildings too. There were also charitable things that needed to be taken care of. An appearance by one of them would go a long way in making more money for the different groups that helped the townspeople.

Caelin was nearly to the drive when he spotted his father

sneaking toward the barns.

Are you ready? He could talk to them all now, and was glad that they said that they were. The only one that he was worried about was Vance of all people, but he knew that he'd come through on this too. He was a warrior, after all. *He comes to you by the barn doors. I know that you're seeing him as I do, but he has a bit of magic that he didn't before. Butler murdered several faeries, and has taken their magic.*

I am so sorry for your loss.

He thought of Micky and told her that he'd taken care that they were resting at peace. She thanked him in the only way she knew how — she said that she would give the earth a little of herself to help with the flowers. It was a very lovely gift, one that he cherished even more because she'd given it so willingly.

Butler moved along the house. He looked upset, and Caelin reached into his head to find out what had bothered him today. The people from the town, he knew, had been giving him a very difficult time of it. Not that he cared, but he had told them to be careful of him. Butler was a sneaky bastard and would hurt anyone that might be around when he was mad.

"So, you think that my flesh and blood would stay in a hotel rather than the castle that belongs to them?" Butler stopped moving and looked around. Caelin showed himself, but stayed away. There was no reason to let him come any closer. "You went to a lot of trouble to find them, I think. As there are only two hotels in town, where else did you think my family to be?"

"They're not your family unless they are also mine. And I do not wish to claim such upstarts. Why are they in my home anyway? And what have they done to it? I want you to tell them to get out. To pack their bags and to leave here this minute." He saw them coming out of the keep but said nothing to Butler. "This is not the way it should be, Caelin. You're my son, and you will obey me."

"Will I? I doubt very much that you even knew my name until someone told it to you." Butler blamed that on his mother. "She was brilliant, I think, in keeping me away from you. There is no telling what sort of person I would have been should you have had a hand in my upbringing."

"You would have been a better man to me, that's what you would have been. And we would have found much more magic than this piddly amount that I found for myself." Caelin asked about the faeries. "Yes, I killed them. What did you expect me to do? Meet with the dragons with nary a thing to protect myself? I am your father, after all. Did you not want me to survive?"

"No. I would like very much if you were to die, actually. As for you killing them, there is a penalty for that. One that I will take from you soon enough." They were all there then, the McCades and their mates. Even the queen, Alisha, was there, and she did not seem happy to see Butler. "What will you do to the McCade men, Butler? You cannot kill them. You have tried before to take their jewelry, and all that got you was more pain and heartache. Not to mention, all your money too. There wasn't much, not as much as you promised people that helped you. But it was never your intention to pay them anyway, was it? You had them die for no other reason than greed."

"Of course I have greed. Every man, woman, and child has greed in their hearts. They just don't admit it as I do. What do you have, Caelin? A fine house that has servants? A pot of gold that you dip into when the need arises? I have nothing." Caelin told him that he deserved nothing. "So says you. But I was king here once, and I will be again. This is my castle. The money here that was left by your mother, it is mine."

"Nay, it is not. As for my pot of gold? No, I have none of that. I have a wife that cares for me deeply. Children, both sons and daughters, who have given me plenty of grandchildren to bounce upon my knees. I have a home that is warm in the winter months, cooler in the hot ones. We have plenty enough food to share with anyone that needs it, as well as enough love to make us happy." Butler made a gagging sound, much like a small child when retching up their dinner. "You do not believe me? Or is it love that you do not believe in?"

"Neither. You have magic galore and you think you're better than me. What will you do with your fine house and lady wife when I am king? How will you live when I take all that you have from you, just as you have me?" Caelin laughed, thinking Butler a fool. "You will not laugh when this all comes true. See if you don't."

"Oh, I shall laugh. All of us shall, won't we?" Butler turned and looked at the people there. He might have seen a few of them around town, but he'd probably not know their names. "Shall I introduce you to my family, Butler? This is Kenton and his wife Emma. She wears the ring that brought

124

the heart to life. Next to them is Jorden and his wife, Jasmine. Jasmine found the earrings in a box of junk, paying only a few dollars for them. Grady there, he inherited the castle from me. His wife Harper wears the arm bands, the torques that were made from the necklace. Dalton and Gabe, his wife, shared the hair combs. They're the color in her hair, the blue of the dragons. Lewis is married to Raven. You remember her, don't you? She's the witch whose mother you killed. You promised her no harm would come to her mother when she helped you become immortal. She can see now, see you for the monster that you are. Then there is Vance. His wife is a faerie, Micky. Micky and Vance are warriors. And true to that, they have the sword that my mother had made for me. The very one that I used to cut into your fatted belly. They have the necklace."

Butler laughed. Caelin made his way to the family, his family, as they stood there watching the man who would be dead soon. Butler opened his shirt, displaying the wound that he'd given him, as well as the fake necklace that he'd worn around his neck since he'd nearly lost it several times.

"As you can see here, I have the necklace. You're a fool if you thought that I'd believe that you had it. I've had it since your whore of a mother left it behind when she fled the castle with you at her side." Caelin watched the men, their dragons, so close to the surface that he wondered how they were holding them. "Your mother is dead now. And if not, she will be soon enough."

"My mother lives, with the spark that will bring forth the dragon. And she didn't lead me away, Butler, but sent me to our place, a place that I'd be safe from you and your ways."

125

Butler laughed again. "You will know soon enough that you have lost. When the dragon comes forth and you are killed."

He grabbed Micky to him. Caelin hadn't seen Butler move, but was aware that at some point he would. As he held her to his body, the long knife at her throat, the dragons showed themselves, their sizes much bigger than he'd thought they'd be.

"Tell them to give it all to me."

The only one that hadn't shifted was Vance, but it was working out the way it should. There was a time for him to come forth, and he would soon enough.

Butler screamed again. "Tell them that they're to give me the jewelry so that I might have the dragon. They have what I want, and if I don't get it, I'll kill her."

No one moved; the dragons seemed to be held back by some magical force. Caelin thought that was about right. The magic of them all needed to be there before they could kill this man. As a small drop of blood slipped from the wound at Micky's throat, he spoke to Vance. It was time.

~~~

Vance called for his dragon, screamed for him to come to him. When nothing happened, not a sound from him, he reached for the sword at his back and pulled it forward. He felt the power of it, all the magic that he'd been ignoring in favor of finding his dragon.

He cannot kill her, my lord. Warrior spoke to him when all he wanted to do was change into something that would save his wife. *He cannot kill her, for she is as immortal as you.*

"I don't understand." Warrior said that he did. "No. I

126

don't. You can't mean for me to stab her so that I can kill him."

No. You cannot kill him that way. You will need to remove his head while he holds your wife. Vance felt like he'd been sucker punched. He wanted him to kill his wife to kill Butler? *She cannot die.*

"You keep saying that. I don't know what you're saying. If you mean that I should remove his head while doing the same to her, then no, I can't kill her to get to him. And if I remove her head, she'll be as dead as I will be without her there with me." Warrior told him again that she could not die. "She will. Removing her head will kill her. It'll kill anyone, and you know it."

"Vance." He looked at Caelin and the woman standing beside him. "My mother has faith in you. I do as well. You must be the one that ends his life — the sword has chosen you to do this."

"No, I won't do it. I won't kill her." Caelin said to trust him. "Trust you? You should have killed him when you had the chance. I won't cut her head off to kill him. No one should be asked to do such a thing."

"Then she will die. As will you all. The child that she now carries, your son, will die with her because Butler will rule, and he will order your deaths. Without the magic of all of you, then nothing you have been given will live either." Vance wanted to scream at him to shut up, he had to think. "You have to trust me."

"I don't have to trust anyone. You just want me to kill her." He knew deep in his heart that wasn't true. Caelin would never make him kill his own wife. Then the queen,

Prisane, came to stand beside him. "I don't want to kill her."

"As my son has said, then all will die." He looked at his brother, large dragons spraying fire on the grasses before them. "The townspeople will die. Everyone will. He will rule the earth, because he'll be able to with the dragon, and there will never be another McCade born to take up the path again."

"You said that it would restart if we didn't kill him. You said that." She told him that she'd not known that the sword had come to him. "What does that have to do with it? Someone else will just take it up."

"No, Vance. If you die, and you will if you don't use it, then the sword will die with you. And that is the only thing that will kill Butler." This was too much. What they were asking him to do, telling him to do, was too much. "Swing the sword at their throats and she will live. This I promise you with all that I am."

He stood there with the sword in his hands. Butler was screaming at them to give the jewelry to him. And he knew that he'd not heard a word said to him, not from Caelin nor the queen. When the blade at Micky's throat cut deeper into her, he knew that he'd have no choice in this. He either tried it their way, or she'd be dead anyway.

Vance gripped the pommel tightly in his hands. The heat coming from it made him think his dragon was finally coming for him. But when he thought of the sword cutting through only Butler's throat, he felt a calmness settle over him.

Swinging the sword back over his shoulder, Vance took the two steps necessary toward them. He looked only at Micky. He mouthed that he loved her and that he was sorry for this. At her nod, she closed her eyes and he swung the sword with all his strength.

Sparks flew off the necklace that was around Micky's neck. Even the sword seemed to shudder at the feeling, like metal hitting metal. The vibration shook his body, and he wasn't sure what had happened until he saw Butler on the ground, with Micky on the ground in front of him.

Now that Butler was no longer holding her, he reached for his bride and pulled her to him. But before he was able to touch her, to bring her to him, the blue of the sparks surrounded her and engulfed her in their brightness.

The sword grew hotter. The ground shook more, and he wasn't sure where to find Micky. Vance thought that the spark was keeping her safe, making her whole again after he'd cut her. But almost as soon as he touched the blue orb that held her, a great dragon came out of it, larger than all his brothers together, and it spewed out fire, white hot, all over Butler as he laid there screaming at them to give him his due.

"Kill him, my love." He could only stare at the dragon that was his wife. She was the spark, the dragon that was brought forth. "Kill him with the sword."

The fire rained down on Butler, but still he lived. He wasn't an immortal as they were, he remembered. So, to end this, he would need his head removed. Drawing the sword up and over his shoulder again, he sliced it through the flames and removed the head of the man who would have killed his only true love.

It was over in a matter of seconds. Butler's head slipped from his body, rolling toward him so that he looked up at him. Vance started to kick it away when the flames poured over him and the head.

He wasn't hurt. Not even warmed up a little. Instead, he watched as the head, along with the body, dried up. There was nothing left when the flame stopped but a small black spot on the ground.

When small arms wrapped around him, Vance pulled Micky to him. Holding her like this was just what he needed as he watched his brothers, one by one, take to the sky. They were a sight to behold, he thought, all the shades of blue circling around and around until they blurred into a large circle.

As they flew over the castle the townspeople came to see them, and a roar of approval rose from them all. It was over. The bastard was dead, and they were all safe from him for the rest of their days.

Sitting down on the ground, suddenly exhausted, Vance lay on his back and looked up at his family. He wasn't sure he could join them, but right now, he didn't care. They were alive, all of them safe, and he had done what he had to do. Not willingly, of course, but he'd done it.

Vance must have closed his eyes. The next thing he knew he was being carried into the castle and laid out on his bed. He didn't even have the energy to thank the person carrying him, but rolled over and let sleep take him once again.

Waking several times, he only raised his head enough to see that he wasn't alone. Sometimes the room was bright with light from the window, and sometimes it was dark in the room. But every time he woke, Micky was there with him, sleeping in the bed or reading a book.

There were people talking when he woke this time. He didn't know the voices because they were hushed. Vance had a feeling that they were talking about what had happened and what would now happen since Butler was no longer around. Vance wondered what would change now. For them all.

"You're awake." He sat up then, looking at his mom as she sat in one of the forever occupied chairs. "I sent Micky for some dinner. She's not left you very much, only when I bully her into it."

His throat was dry, and it took him two tries to speak. "I bet that went over well. How is everyone? They're all safe, right?"

"They're all fine. We've been worried about you, but we were assured that using the sword for the first time would drain you. Something about it having to get to know you before you could become one person. I'm not sure how that works, but you'll understand once you're up and about."

"How long have I been here? I'm assuming a few days." She told him he'd been here for ten. "Ten days? No wonder you were worried. And why I'm so hungry."

"Yes, the cook and her staff have been getting ready for you to wake to feed you. Also, the people of the village have been coming by almost hourly to check on you and to leave a token. I had no idea that was a tradition when you killed a slayer, but then I'm new to this whole dragon thing." She laughed as she laid her knitting down. "I always believed my boys were born for great things. But I never would have thought they'd be the ones to find the jewelry. And you? You killed the monster."

"I think that.... Is Micky a dragon?" She laughed and told him that Warrior took her body when he needed it. "So, he'll take a person when he needs one? I don't understand."

"You have a great deal to hear, I'm afraid. We've been figuring things out a little at a time. Apparently, with you being down as long as you were, the queen, Prisane, and Caelin have been resting as well. Caelin's son came to tell us that his father is doing well, and his mom is taking care of him. They've been waiting on you to wake."

"I need a shower. And my wife. Not necessarily in that order, either." Mom stood up and came to him. After kissing him on the forehead, then his cheek, she walked to the door. "I love you, Mom."

"And I love you as well, Vance. And I've never been prouder of my boys than I am right now. All of you, good boys and greater men." She left him there, and he got up to take a long-needed shower. As soon as he was done, he walked into his bedroom to not only find Micky on his bed, but she was naked as well.

"I think the talk will have to wait." She laughed and reached for him. "I'm so glad that you're all right. I don't know what I'd do without you."

Vance had everything that he would ever need, right there.

Chapter 9

They were all seated in the living room when Prisane showed up. She wasn't wholly herself yet, and wouldn't be until a daughter was born to Grady and Harper. The child would be all that she was and more. The daughter would be the greatest witch ever born, and would bring their kind to a new level of magic.

She could walk into a room now instead of just appearing; it was strange now, after being ghost-like for so many decades. And touching things had been a great treat for her as well. But seeing her son after all this time was the best thing that she'd ever had happen. Touching him had been the first thing she'd done when she'd realized that she could, and whenever they were in a room together, she would hold him to her for as long as he'd allow her. Men were such babies when it came to giving their moms hugs. Clearing her throat, she looked around the room at them all.

"I've come to talk to you about things. I'm sure that you all have questions. And I will answer them so that you understand what is to happen now. There are things that I don't know, I must admit. As you have all been told, several times, no generation has ever made it this far. And there are things that we didn't know at all until now." Vance asked about the sword, which was still with him. "That will be yours forever. And when you have a son, your first born, he will have one as well. As will each first-born son that comes to your sons, and so on down the line through all the generations. But the magic that you hold, it is yours only."

"I don't have a dragon, either." Prisane shook her head and told him that was one of the things they hadn't known. "I'll never have one then. Not like my brothers, I guess."

Vance looked sad, she thought. Before this, he'd always looked strained to her, on edge. As if he was under too much pressure for a man his age. While sadness at the news was on his face, she could also tell that he was happier than he'd ever been, and that he was taking strides in making a life for himself outside the service.

"No, you will not have a dragon. But there is a reason for that as well. The Sword of Caelin came to you and took your dragon, for the strength of him and the magic. You were gifted the armor of the sword when you were given it. When the dragons need you or you them, then it will be your job to protect them when they cannot. And vice versa when you need them. You are forever the man who will protect them. As will your son and his son. Have you seen it yet? The armor?"

"No. I mean, I'm not even sure how I'd do that." Prisane

134

looked at Jorden. Jorden laughed and got up to leave them. When he returned, he had the large canvas that she'd seen him working on just that morning. "Is this how I'm going to see it? Through a painting?"

"Sort of. There will be more magic coming your way, and with that, you'll have the ability to see all manner of things. But this is the painting that your brother did of you all. One that I hope will hang here with the rest of the family portraits that were hidden away for you all." She looked at them all again. "You are such a handsome group of men. Some of you look so much like my family members that are long gone. Others look like me, and some Caelin in the mix. And your wives have added a level of beauty that I could never have foreseen."

The sheet was taken off the painting, and she could see that he'd done more to it since she'd seen it. The castle was complete, and the flags of her family now took flight over the turrets. They all stood in front of the painting as Jorden explained.

"When I first had the idea to paint us all, I only wanted to put us, as couples, together on here to give to Mom. The castle was in ruin when I started, and there were only the three of us with wives. So, as I worked on it, only putting us on here and leaving space for the women who would join us, the painting took on a life of its own." He set the canvas up on the mantel of the fireplace. "If you look at us, the men, you can see that we change. You don't have to do anything different, just look at us."

Prisane knew what they were seeing. The dragons of the

wives were there with them. All save one. Vance wasn't a dragon, but he and Micky were in full armor, the armor of her time that looked regal on them. And on the chest piece of them both was the crest that had been on the front of the castle since her father's father had designed it. The crest of a dragon spread out in all his glory. Kenton asked who would see it like this, with them as their other selves.

"Anyone that believes in magic and dragons. Not necessarily both, but one or the other will show them that magic is here, within this house, and that dragons reside here as well." She watched Alisha, who hadn't gone to see the painting, and knew that she'd not be their queen for much longer. She didn't want the job, but wanted to be with her family. "You wish to step down, my lady?"

"I do. I've thought about it a great deal after speaking to Caelin. It does sound like a job that I would enjoy, but I think about my grandchildren, and I want to be with them as well. Gavin has given me so much and I love him dearly, but I think of all the fun that we can have now, and I just don't see that happening while trying to keep dragons from being killed." Prisane nodded. "What do I have to do? I'm sure it's not as easy as just saying that I don't want to be the queen of dragons."

"It is. You only have to find someone to replace you." She looked at Emma when Prisane did. "She will make a fine queen, my lady. And she will be with her king. There is little that they won't be able to do together. You would have done a grand job of it too, but your heart belongs to another, and Gavin is a lucky young man to have you."

Nodding, Alisha said she'd talk to Emma later, but she was sure that she'd take the job. So was Prisane. She had spoken to her recently, and knew that she would only take it if Alisha no longer wanted to do the job. Emma thought that Alisha would want to do it for a long time, but Prisane knew better. She was a woman who needed her grandchildren to love. It was as much a part of her as her heart and lungs, to be able to love someone.

When they rejoined them, Prisane explained about Warrior. Kenton wanted to know if he was still there; no one had seen him since the day Butler had died. Died. Like he'd gone to bed that night and not woken. But they were dealing with a great deal, and she didn't say that he'd deserved what he'd gotten. Instead, she answered the question.

"He was trapped, no other word for it, for such a long time that he needed to stretch himself out. To see things that he otherwise missed. And he did miss a great deal. Also, I think that he is planning to stay here with the family. He has been a part of their lives for so long, he wants to live with them now." Everyone understood, and then Grady stood up. "You wish to say something more to this, Lord Grady?"

"Yes. We've talked it over with the family, everyone including my mom, and we're going to stay here as well. Not that we won't visit home, but we're not going to live there any longer. The others have decided to purchase homes here, so that they can visit often, but Harper and I are going to make our life here." Alisha said she was going to stay as well, to help with the new businesses. "My mom will travel a great deal between the homes. And we're hoping that someday

137

soon, they'll all have permanent homes here."

Kenton cleared his throat before standing too, with Emma by his side. "We've talked it over most of the night, and we too are going to stay. We'll visit home, of course, but we've decided to make this our place to live." Kenton grinned. "If you don't mind all of us being here too."

"Oh, this is wonderful." She looked at the others, the other families that she'd come to love as her own, and they were nodding. "You're all staying here too? Really?"

"Yes. We had decided to simply go back and forth for a while, but then we thought of all that we would miss." Vance looked at Micky as he continued. "There is nothing there for us anymore. With most of the family living here, we decided that we'd start fresh here too. Micky wants to be a lawyer, and I'm thinking of becoming a teacher. Someone to help people defend themselves against bullies and the like."

"We all have to return, however, and soon. Each of us have businesses to see to and take care of for the future. I have a restaurant that is running well even without me there that I have to sell. Or give away. I've not decided as yet." Raven hit Lewis and he laughed as he continued. "I'm giving it away. To someone with a bright future in running a restaurant of her own."

Prisane was so happy that she cried. They would all be here whenever she wanted to speak to them. And when the child was born, she'd be right there with her, her confidant and protector. She hugged them all and sat down again. It was too much for her, to make sure they knew how she felt about their decisions, but she wouldn't have done anything different at all.

"You won't have to purchase homes. There are enough here for all of you. And they're large homes as well, for all the children that will be coming. The estate owns them, which means that you all own them together. You sort it out and I'll have Caelin take care of the paperwork." She cried a little more. "You have no idea how happy you've made me. And how happy Caelin is going to be. He was just saying how he would miss you all when you left."

"I'd like to know what the riches are. Not that I want anything for what we've done. I think, as a group, we've gained so much more than you could ever pay us with. But I don't think it's money, is it? Butler seemed to think that it was all money, gold and coin, he called it. But it's not, I don't think." She shook her head at Dalton, then nodded. "Just like a McCade, as clear as mud when answering a question."

"If you'd like to come with me, I can show it to you. And the place that my son was hidden away for so long. It's a safe place, but a little chilly." They all grabbed what they needed, and she let Caelin know where they were headed. He told her that he'd meet them all there. "Caelin will take over showing you the area once we are there. I have used up about all of my energy for one day. I'll need to learn to pace myself better, I'm afraid."

They followed her to the back of the property, where the lake was still as breathtaking as it had ever been. Prisane told them how it was well stocked, and that the cook usually fished for dinner when there was anything like that on the menu for the night. She smiled when one of the larger fish took that opportunity to leap from the water before splashing back down into it.

Prisane was worn out by the time they got to the other side of the lake. Caelin could see it too when he joined them, and told her that he'd take over. She hugged him again and then a second time before making her way to the place where she'd been for all her years. The cave had served her well as a place to rest, and Warrior was there too.

"I wish to rest with you beside me, my lady." She was glad for it, and when he started a small fire to keep her warm, she snuggled around him and closed her eyes. "How I wish that I could hold you like a man does. You have owned my heart since the first time I saw you, my lady."

"And you mine, my Warrior. Had I been able to keep you as a man, we would have been so happy, the three of us. But alas, it cannot be." Tears fell from his eyes and she picked up the beautiful diamond. "Tears of love make emeralds, tears of heartache make diamonds. I love you too, so very much."

~~~

The path took them below the lake. Vance wasn't thrilled about being under something so heavy, but as soon as he saw what treasures were hidden away, he forgot about the weight of the water just above them. Instead, he marveled at all that was there.

"My mom and the dragon moved most of this down here before I was born. The paintings that are over there in that corner I was able to get back from the people Butler sold them to for little cash. He also took some tapestries and a few plates and such, but I've not been able to find them. I will, I

140

hope, but it's taken me a long time, so I think they might be lost to me." Caelin showed them the trunks. "These are filled with seeds and spices. My mother has a good head on her shoulders, and knew that someday these would be hard to find. Also, you'll find that the orchard on the estate is filled with all kinds of trees and such that shouldn't be growing here. The entire place is filled with magic that we give back to it every time we take something away."

"Take from the earth, feed it ten times the amount." Caelin nodded at Micky and smiled. "I've had my own share of taking from the earth over the years, so I'm glad to hear that it's still a practice."

"It is. And you'll see that every farmer here does the same. We know that we have a bounty here, and we go to great strides to keep the earth happy." Vance walked to the wall that seemed to hold nothing but wrapped items. When he picked up the first one, he looked at Caelin when he laughed. "My mother loved swords. And these are all the ones that she had commissioned over the decades before my father. Each of them have been used in war or in practice. Even I have used them on occasion to keep up with my skills. Those are all yours, Vance. When you chose a home, I'll make sure that they're given to you."

"This is too much." Caelin said that it wasn't, not for what he'd given them. "But these swords are worth a fortune. Aren't you afraid of something happening to them? Or that someone will take them?"

"No one here will steal from you unless they are hungry or in need. Instead of having them arrested or turned away, we feed them, cloth them if they need that as well. But we all care for anyone that needs it." Caelin handed him another sword, this one more beautiful than the first. "The other day I saw a man and his children stealing from a garden. Instead of turning him away as people you know would have, I brought them to my home. My wife, she bathed the children and dressed them in some of the things that are forever there, and we all ate dinner together. The next day he tells me that he can work for me. And he does now. He is a teacher that is showing younger children how to preserve and take care of our trees and land. Everything you do, it has a return on it, whether it be bad or good. Understand?"

"I do. I really do." They wandered around the large area. Vance went to one of the walls to see what was holding it up and was surprised to see that it was only stone. Small and large ones that were held together by mud. He then realized how much time it would have taken for something like this to be put together. The forethought on how it would work. "Your mother is more than smart, I think. But brilliant."

"And magical. We cannot forget that. Most of what was done here was by magic. It's held up over the decades much better than even I thought it would. We've had no trouble with it, not even from the lake above it. But as with the earth, we give to her as well." Vance was beginning to see how insignificant he was in the larger scheme of things. "You're not. I can read your mind, but I didn't have to. What you are thinking is written on your face. You, of all the brothers, were the most important part of all this. Yes, the dragons were needed from time to time, and will be again, but you were the one that had to end this."

"Because I'd seen death before. Because of what I am." Caelin said he was just a man to him. "No, you know what I mean. I'm a man who has committed and seen a great deal of death."

"That had nothing to do with it. Well, perhaps a little, but you would have been the one no matter what the circumstances would have been with what you did. You have the bravest heart of them all. And believe it or not, the purest." Vance shook his head. "No, you do. Your heart has never been touched by anyone with greed in their heart. Neither have the others, but you were stronger than them in so many ways. And wielding the sword, mine and my mother's sword, would not have done what it needed when it needed to for anyone but you. None of them could have broken the diamond that freed the dragon. As well as being marked as you have been."

"Marked?" Caelin nodded at him and pulled up his own sleeve. There was a dragon from his shoulder to his elbow, and his tail curled around his wrist to be in his palm. "I don't have that."

Caelin took his hand in his, the one with the dragon on it. As soon as he touched him, Vance fell to the floor—the pain was incredible. He heard Micky screaming as well, and knew that whatever he was getting, she was as well. But Vance knew that his mark, because that was what it was, was going to be larger and bigger than Micky's. When the pain subsided, he stood again and told his brothers he was all right.

"That wasn't nice, I know, but I had to see first if the dragon would take you. I was afraid that if he didn't go to you and your mate, you'd worry again. You worry a great deal, don't you?" Caelin laughed and Vance wanted to slug him. But he was slightly afraid to. "As you should be. I have given you what I am, Vance. The warrior for the dragons."

"Why?" He pulled his shirt off and looked down at his body. "Christ, it's huge, isn't it? Look at the color on it as well."

"She's much larger than mine is, yes. The color means that you're the last of the warriors. When you have a son, he'll take on some of your sigil, but not all. He will be a warrior too, but not as brave nor as strong as you." Vance felt it move over his skin, and when the head of the dragon was on his chest, it seemed to look up at him. "She knows what you are as well. And when you need her, she'll come from your body, much like Roderick and his mate do from the others."

It moved again, this time from his chest to his waist, and curled around him. It didn't hurt, not at all, but it was as if he had a belt on that was slightly too tight. Almost as soon as he thought that, the dragon moved again, and it wasn't nearly as tight as it had been. Micky joined him and showed him her dragon.

"As with all things, there is a balance. You have a male on you, Lady Micky, and Lord Vance a female. The two of you will forever be the warriors of the dragons." Caelin moved away then, and went to talk to Emma, who was looking at the pictures with Jorden.

"Did you ever think we'd have a dragon on our bodies?" Vance held Micky in his arms and told her no. "The baby approves, I think. Just as I was taken to the ground, I felt him move. It's a son."

"Yes, I think I might have dreamed that the night you conceived." Micky looked up at him. "We're to name him Caelin Vance McCade. And he'll name his first born the same. We'll have a great many of them, too."

"I love that." She held him, and he kissed the top of her head. "There is a house in town that I'd like to purchase for us. If it's not part of the estate. It's a grand old home that has seven bedrooms, as well as a large barn on the property. It's going to need a little work, but I think we can get it done."

"Anything you wish, I'll try my best to get it for you." She looked at him again. "You have given me a world with love in it. Something that I never dreamed, much less thought would be mine. And now that we're going to have a child, I couldn't be any happier. And every day with you is like a gift that I will treasure as much as the things here in this cellar."

The rest of the afternoon was spent going through the crates of things that had been put here. Some of the paintings, as well as other things, were set aside for each of them to take to their homes. His swords were with the things that Micky had picked out, as well as several large crates and trunks. His pile was considerably smaller than the rest, but she assured him that they had what they wanted. Vance told her he just didn't want to carry it anywhere.

"Caelin, I'd like to talk to you about a house here in town. The grand one that is on the main street. At the end, Micky told me." Caelin told him that it was his if he wanted it. "No, I want to buy it. Even if it is a part of the estate, there should be money for it."

"No, not from family. And I'm glad to see you going into that one. The mayor used to live there at one time, so it has all the bells and whistles, I think you call it." They both laughed. "Will you consider being our mayor, Vance? We could use a good man like you; someone that has seen the worst in people, and the good."

"I don't know. That seems like a job for someone that knows the area better than I do." Caelin just laughed. "You know something that I should, don't you?"

"Your office is already set up in the courthouse. And I believe stationary has been printed for you as well. As soon as you killed Butler and released the dragon, the people took a vote, not with my knowledge, and said that you were to be the mayor. And your wife, she'll be very helpful to you in projects that need to be taken care of."

"I think I've been bamboozled." They both laughed, and he realized that he really did want the job as mayor. It was something that he'd never thought of, like a great many things that he had now, but he knew that he could make it work. With Micky at his side. "You know, I have to talk to Micky, but I would like the job, I think. So long as they really want me there after six months. I might be a total screw up with it."

"I doubt very much that you've ever screwed anything up in your life, but you talk to Micky and I'll tell the people. They might come pounding at your door, so I'd hurry if I were you."

Vance found Micky looking at stacks of plates. She and Emma were trying to decide if they were priceless heirlooms or just everyday ones to use in the castle. He didn't think that it really mattered, but kept his mouth shut. When his mom came to stand by him, Vance wrapped his arm around her and kissed her cheek. He had missed her a great deal over the years he'd been away and was glad that she was going to be close. He looked over at Micky as something occurred to him.

"We're going to have a baby." She hugged him tightly, and he smiled at her when she started to cry. "Will you come and live with us? I mean, all the time. I just got a house that I've never seen, and Micky is happy. I'd like to make up for the time that I missed with you."

"What will Micky say about this? You should talk to her first." He realized that she hadn't said no, and that gave him heart. "Talk to your wife and we'll see."

"Talk to me about what?" Vance told Micky what he'd heard from Caelin and about the house. Then he told her that he would like for his mom to stay with them forever. "Oh yes, that would be the greatest thing to ever happen to us. Say you'll do it, Alisha. If you do, I'd love to call you Mom. Not blackmail, mind you. I was going to ask you about that anyway, but please come and live with us. It'll help me so much with the baby, cooking, and such."

"How could I turn you down? Yes, I'd love that. If you're sure." They both nodded and she hugged them both. "I have so much right now, more than I ever dreamed was possible."

"Yes, I feel the same way." He held the two women that meant the world to him, one on each side, and hugged them. Vance was happy. Mayor of a new town, and about to be a father. He loved his life.

Vance told Caelin that he wanted the job and that his mom

was going to be staying with him. The others were happy, but jealous. Kenton pouted like a small boy, but Mom told him she'd come and stay the night sometimes. Vance picked up Micky and swung her around before setting her on the floor and kissing her.

"I love you, Mrs. McCade, dragon warrior, wife to the new mayor." She laughed, and he loved her even more. "I can't wait to see you large with our baby, love. I just cannot wait."

Chapter 10

Alisha thought that the trip back home was depressing. She knew that they were all going back in less than a month, but she'd not wanted to leave. While she understood there were things that had to be done at home, she didn't want to do it. Things were going nicely for her, and she loved that.

The house that the boys had grown up in was really too large for her anyway. And since their father had lived there with her when he was around, it didn't mean as much to her as when she was there with her sons. Her sons were her entire world.

Making a list of things that needed to be taken care of, comparing it to the ones that the others were making, she realized that it would be easier to just sell it all with the house and be done with it. There were things that she wanted, but nothing that she couldn't live without. The only thing that really was near her heart was the box of ornaments that she'd put each of the things that the boys had made her or given her to hang on the tree.

She was in the attic when Jasmine joined her. She was large with child, and Alisha worried about her, but she assured her that she was just fine. Sitting in the rocking chair that had been around since Kenton was born, she rocked slowly as she started talking about the home they were in.

"I need to talk to you about something." Alisha said she was there for her. "I know that. I've always known that. But I'm to understand that you're planning to sell the house and all the contents."

"Yes. I've been a penny pincher all my life, and even with the money that we have, I saw no reason to go out and buy all new. Besides, most of this stuff is fairly old and still in good shape." Jasmine smiled and nodded. "Why do I have the feeling that you're going to tell me not to sell?"

"Oh no, I want you to, but with my stuff. I got in contact with a friend of Emma's. Doesn't she know just about everyone in some sort of business? Anyway, she has a friend that buys furniture for television and movie sets. You know, to make it in a time period that they're shooting for. They want to come and have a look at my shop. And I'm going to bring them here, to see if they want any of these things if you don't mind." Alisha said she didn't mind at all. "Good. I was hoping you'd say that. He's downstairs."

"Now?" Jasmine nodded. "My goodness, child, you certainly do work fast. I'd be able to keep a few things, right?"

"Oh yes. He's very clear about that. He'll have a look around, think about it, then make you an offer on all the pieces that he'll give you a list for. He bought my store out, Alisha. Every stick of furniture. All the pictures, lacey things, as well as the curtains. He said that he'd be able to use it at some point, and he's very excited to have it." As they made their way down the stairs, careful of them, Jasmine told her about how he had all kinds of projects that would use the things. "Rob, this is my mother-in-law, Alisha McCade. Alisha, this is Rob James. He owns and operates Just Perfect."

"Hello, my dear. Oh, what a lovely home you have here. I just love it all. The setting, the trees around the back. Even the pool. Does it work? No matter, we can have someone fix it. I'll take it all." Alisha looked at Jasmine, then back at Rob. "You are selling your home, correct? I didn't just make a major mistake, did I?"

"No, I'm selling my home as well as everything but a few items in it. I guess I'm confused. You want what all? And what does this have to do with the pool? Which does work, by the way. I have it cleaned up and refilled every year for the boys." He nodded, the grin on his face almost splitting his face in two. "You're very happy, I can tell that, but I just don't understand."

"I can use this house in several movies and television shows that are set in this time frame. I love that you've kept it up, but not gotten rid of the beauty of the home. The hardwood floors. Even the fireplace is perfect. The wraparound porch is absolutely divine, and I think that once I go up to the upper floors, I'm going to find that it's in the same perfect condition. All preserved for me." Nodding, still unsure of what he was talking about, he asked her to have a seat. "I'm getting entirely too far ahead of myself here. You see, I not only find pieces for movies, but also homes that can be used. The inside as well as just the outside. We might not ever use the indoors of some homes — the people still live there or something. But we pay them to use the image of their place for the shows. Understand?"

"I do. Yes. You want to use the outside of my home. I'm afraid you'll have to take that up with the person who will buy this home. I'm selling it." He nodded and said he was buying it. "The house and the contents? You want it all?"

"Oh my yes. There is so much we can use in this house. The outside of it is just one of the many things that we can use. And each room will be used for something else. Say a bedroom for a family member. The kitchen, which is used a great deal, can be setup like a home from the early thirties." He handed her a list. "These are the items that I need for five upcoming projects. As you can see, you have all but one of them, right here. And Jasmine has been able to supply me with the rest."

"I need a box from the attic. And my clothing. Not all of it, just a few things to tide me over." He said he'd take it all, but anything she wanted, he'd be glad to part with it if she sold the rest to him. "Yes. Yes, you've saved me a great deal of time. Thank you so much. I'm slightly overwhelmed. I was just thinking about how I didn't want to do this, go through the hassle of selling it all. And now you've taken that task all away from me. I might have to stay in a hotel before we're ready to leave town."

"You'll stay with us." Jasmine hugged her tightly. "Thanks,

Rob. It's been fantastic meeting you. As soon as the family attorney goes over the contract, you can take possession. He'll also need to go over Alisha's."

"Yes, I completely understand. But I must thank you ladies for helping me. You have no idea how happy I am that you called me. My goodness, I'll have to send a dozen or so roses to Miss Emma. She is a wonderful person, and I was so glad that she got out from under her brother's influence. Poor girl."

After he left them, with a contract in hand, Alisha sat on the couch and had to take a small breather. Jasmine laughed and asked her if she was all right. Nodding, she looked at her daughter-in-law and realized just how much she loved her daughters.

"I have to confess something to you. I've been down a bit lately. Since before we went to the castle and took care of that man." She refused to say his name, giving him power. "I was thinking that I'd try to talk to someone that could take my immortality away and let me go in peace. I just felt...well, I guess you could say that I felt like odd man out. All my boys have wives now. And you all do such a wonderful job of keeping them happy. I don't, however, feel happy."

"You still feel that way?" Alisha started to tell her that she didn't, but she also didn't want to lie, so she told her that she felt like that every single day. "I'm sorry, Alisha. I am. But I have to tell you that if not for you being around all the time, I think I'd go insane. You are such a joy to us all. And Jorden and I are hoping that you'll come stay with us a few days after the baby is born. I know that I have Gavin, and—

Oh my goodness, have you any idea how much he'll be hurt if you leave him? I've never seen a kid have so much fun with someone like he does you. And I know you and he are like co-conspirators. I think, if he could, he'd be living with you all the time instead of just spending most of his time with you."

"He is such a joy to me. But he really should be hanging out with boys his own age." Jasmine asked her if she knew any boys his age that were as smart as him. "Honey, I don't think kids my age are as smart as he is. He's sort of scary smart, isn't he?"

"Yes. And he wants to be an attorney. Gavin thinks that the family will need one because we'll never die. He seems to think that we'll be getting into a lot of trouble." Alisha laughed with her. "I have an idea. Why not go to college too? You could become anything you wanted. Or ever dreamed of becoming. It's not like you have to work, but it would be kind of fun, I think, to have a hobby to figure out and learn all there is to know about it."

Going to college at her age? It was something to think about, she supposed. Maybe she could get her business degree. Something that she could do that would be useful. Alisha looked at Jasmine. The woman was smiling again, and Alisha fell in love with her, like her own flesh and blood daughter.

They talked a bit more, and then Jasmine said that she had to get the contracts to their attorney. It would be a couple of days, Jasmine told her, and she should use that time to figure out what she wanted for the house. Alisha thanked her again and went to the living room.

She looked around the big room. There were a lot of memories in this one. The Christmases they'd had in here. They had been so wonderful, but there was also the day that she'd killed her husband. The stain was still there, the wood also marred by the axe that he'd dropped when she'd done it.

He'd been such an abusive man. Even when they were first married, she'd been afraid of him. But when they had come together, as a favor to both families, it had been a time when there weren't divorces, nor did anyone talk about the abuse one might have in a family. So, she had endured.

Then the boys started coming along. They had been her saving grace, as well as her biggest fear. She never wanted them to be hurt by their father, and she tried very hard to hide from them what sort of person he was. But they weren't stupid, and from such a young age they knew that he was hurting her.

It made them better men, she thought. To see how much he had hurt her, even when he was only abusing her. But when he'd gone after one of her boys, that was it for him. She simply pulled out the gun she'd been carrying for several weeks and shot him right in the head with it.

Lewis had been caught in the middle because he was trying to protect her. She was sure that if any of the others had been there, one of them would have been the one he had held down and tried to make her do what he wanted. She remembered it just like it had happened only hours ago instead of all those years.

"You'll come here and let me have you, or he's dead. And then I'll take you anyway, Alisha. You're my wife and you'll

155

do as I say." Lewis didn't scream or cry, but watched her. Alisha told Kent that was his son, he couldn't hurt him. "I will if you don't do what I tell you. And while you're standing there thinking, you remember where you put any money that you got yourself squirreled away. I need that too."

"No. The boys need it. They're in school now, and they need things." Kent laughed and said he was tired of them kids draining them, and he might just end them all. "You will not. They're my boys."

"You'd not have them if it weren't for me. Now get your ass in gear, Alisha, and get me that money. Then you be ready for me. I have shit I need to get done. I might even leave you with another kid to make up for the ones you're going to lose today because you're a fucking bitch." The gun came out as if it had done it on its own. "What do you think you're going to do with that? You think to wound me, Alisha? Won't stop me. If you think it will, you might as well kill me dead. I'll hurt you if you don't."

She aimed it and shot. When he fell back, the axe narrowly missing Lewis, she gathered her son up and held him until the police arrived. Before they could get there, the others had come home and sat with her on the couch. It was the only time in her life that she felt like she'd done something wrong. And that turned out all right too.

~~~

Vance felt like he was going to prison. He wasn't—he just hated being in his dress blues, as they were called. As he shined his shoes again on the back of his pant leg, he thought of all the things he'd rather be doing than sitting here waiting for an interview with the president. Acting president, he remembered.

Why he wanted to see him was a mystery, after Vance telling him that he'd had enough of Army life. He had a wife, and a child on the way, and that was it for him. Vance even told him that he had another job lined up, and that he was excited to be starting a new venture in his life. But he had insisted, and when anyone with the name President of the United States in any part of their title said they wanted to meet you, you had to meet with them.

"Sergeant McCade? Can I get you anything to drink? I'm sorry his meeting is running over. I don't think he's very happy about it either." He told her he was fine, then asked if he should just come back. "No, he asked that you wait. It won't be too much longer."

He'd been told that twice now. Vance pulled at his necktie and leaned back in the seat. He wanted to be with Micky today. They'd decided that since they were in town, they'd see a play, go to a nice restaurant, and have some fun. Not that they'd not have fun where they were going, but today was going to be the final chapter of his life in the Army.

Selling his house had been much easier than he'd thought it would be. There was an influx of new businesses going in, and one of the people that had a nice restaurant elsewhere in the world had decided to buy Dragon's Lair, as well as his home to live in. The man hadn't even dicked around with the pricing but paid what he said, and had already had his financing cleared.

He and Micky were going to celebrate in grand style

today, if he ever got out of here. Additionally, he wanted to do some shopping, deciding just last night when he saw the rings on his other sisters-in-laws' fingers, he wanted to get Micky a ring.

Not just any ring either. He had called a jeweler that lived here and had them make him something that he'd seen in a dream he'd had. It was going to be beautiful, he hoped, and with the gems that he'd gotten from the castle, he was sure it was going to be something that Micky would love it too.

"Sergeant, the president will see you now." He stood up and tried to fix his tie again and thought fuck it, he was here on time and had had to wait. He'd just have to see him as he was. "He said that I'm to bring you a whiskey, is that all right with you?"

"No thanks. I don't drink. But a water would be fantastic, please." She nodded and left him at the door. Knocking once, he entered the room when he heard that he could enter. Kirk Delaney was sitting behind a large desk, and his entire family was there as well. "What's going on here?"

"It's harder than you think it is to do something without the paper knowing all about it. But I managed to pull it off, and I think I did a hell of a job of it too." Vance nodded, but was still confused when Kirk stood up, coming to him. "I didn't think you'd want a lot of fanfare with this. You're a man that does his job, does it well, and gives credit where credit is due. I wanted to thank you for that."

"It was my job, sir." He looked at his wife and his mom, sitting on the couch like being in the Oval Office was an everyday thing. "What is it I won't want any fanfare for?"

"I'm giving you a Medal of Honor." Vance thought he'd heard him wrong and asked him to repeat it. "The Medal of Honor. I'm as sure as I'm standing here that you probably not only feel you don't deserve it, but you also can't think of a single reason that I should be giving you this. You see, I've had a long look at your service record. The one that no one else but me can see."

"You're right, on both accounts." He pulled at his tie again, and then saw his mom huff at him. "I don't usually get this dressed up to come in and tell anyone that I don't care to work for them, Mom."

"You look very handsome. I don't think I've seen you look like this since you graduated from the Army all those years ago." She fixed his tie for him and then touched some of the medals that he had had to put on this morning before leaving the hotel. "These have no meaning to me. As I'm sure they don't to you either. All I ever cared about was having you home safely when you could get there. But the president, Kirk, was telling us some of the things you'd been doing when away. And I have to tell you son, I'm so happy that I didn't know. I would have worried myself into an early grave."

"I was only doing my job." He looked at his family and told them again how he'd only done what he'd been told. "So to be honored with this, it's too much."

"No, I don't think it is. And you didn't always do your job, did you, son?" He glanced at Kirk, then looked at his mom as he continued. "Had you only done what you were told, we'd be at war now. Or something much worse. The country would be in shambles. The arms that we were sending over

159

there would have killed our own men, thanks to the others in office. No, I think that you of all people deserve this medal more than anyone I can think of right now. You saved us. And a great many people like you."

His family shook his hand and Micky came to stand beside him as the President showed them the medal he was going to pin on him. Vance wasn't sure if he deserved it or not, but it looked to him like it was a done deal. So he stood there like a good soldier and waited for Kirk to do it.

"The Medal of Honor is the United States' highest and most prestigious military decoration. It's for the men and women that have distinguished themselves by acts of valor and bravery." Vance watched him as he was decorated once again, and felt more pride in this one than any other because his mom and wife were here. "Command Sergeant Major Vance McCade."

"I'm sorry, what was that?" His mom looked at him as he spoke; he wasn't sure that the new acting president knew what he was saying. "I'm Retired Sergeant Vance McCade, not command sergeant major. If so, I've skipped quite a few ranks in there."

He laughed, hoping that someone would laugh with him. When Kirk only shook his head, smiling at him the whole while, Vance shook his head too, telling him that it wasn't right. He was retired.

"Perhaps to you, you're retired, but to myself, along with most of the people that now work for me, you're never going to retire, and you'll be paid accordingly. The promotion should have happened a long time ago." He said that there

160

were others, his men that were dead now too. "Yes, I've taken care that each family that was left behind has been told what a great man their husband, father, and brother was. Also, they're being given a nice check to help them with the day to day of living without their loved one. I cannot tell you how sorry I am that this hasn't been taken care of before now, Vance. But it's been a privilege for me to be able to bestow this honor on a man who deserves this and so much more."

He shook his hand, then they hugged. It was an honor for him too, Vance told him, to be able to do what he'd done in order to make things right for a lot of people. The medal would forever stay on the uniform, and he'd show it to his children someday, he supposed.

Vance had never told his family what he'd been doing when he was away. He supposed in a way they might have known some of it. He was forever hurt in some way, and when something happened that he'd been a part of, he could come home for a few days. One or more of his family would comment on an event that took place, never asking him about it, but he had a feeling they knew in some way. That their brother and his team had not just caused the outcome of whatever had happened, but also killed whatever got in their way when they did it.

"Are you all right with all this?" He asked Micky if there was more coming. "Just dinner with him upstairs. He didn't want to put your picture in the paper—he was afraid you'd hunt him down. You wouldn't do that, would you?"

Vance just winked at her and she laughed. "I don't hunt down people just for a picture. Besides, I know just where he

161

is at all times. So that makes it easier."

He could tell that she didn't know if he was kidding or not. Which he supposed was what made him so good at his job—the ability to make people believe anything he wanted them to.

When the sword stirred at his back, he looked around the room. There was nothing out of the ordinary, but something was off. As the feeling got stronger, he started reaching out to the people in the room, his family, telling them that something was wrong. Just as he was making his way to the president, he felt the sting of a bullet crease his arm just as he leapt at him, taking Kirk to the ground.

As he was going down, his head hitting the desk, he wondered briefly if things would ever be just quiet and calm. But holding the man down proved to be harder than he thought when the Secret Service decided to fucking do their job.

Things got just a little chancy there for a minute or two. He was sure that the men who were supposed to be protecting Kirk were going to shoot him. Then his mom stepped in to the fray and slapped the first man she came to. The agent didn't blink an eye, and had started to turn his gun on her when Kenton stepped in and took the man to the floor.

Vance had to laugh every time he saw the agent's face after it was cleaned up. The agent kept staring at his mom and brother like he'd love nothing more than to kill them both. But he was in handcuffs as well, having pulled his gun on a civilian. Vance thought the man was lucky that he'd not ended up in a body bag, as the man had that shot him.

The man who had shot into the room they were in had been killed by a sniper. He'd been taken away within minutes; no one would be the wiser of what had happened. Things like this, small things that could be contained, were put away but not forgotten. Vance was positive that someone would lose their job over this one. Including the agent.

The rest of the people, mostly the entire wing they were in, had been put on lockdown for a little while longer, just to make sure that there wasn't anyone else in the building or on the lawns. His wound was looked at, but he insisted that he was fine. By the time he was taking off his jacket to be cleaned and repaired, the wound was as if it had never been.

"You saved my life." Vance said nothing as they were escorted up to the family wing and seated for dinner. "I can't...I honestly don't know what to say. You saved my life, and I'm indebted to you greatly. And if you tell me you were only doing your job, I might hurt you again. Christ, that person meant to kill me."

"No, sir, he didn't." Kirk looked at Raven when she sat down beside him. "He only meant to scare you. Not that it makes it any better, but he never meant to kill you. He wanted you to recognize that no matter who is president, they can always be gotten to. If I were you, I'd fire the entire group of agents with you now and get your own. They were very loyal to the previous regimen."

"They had a part in this?" She only stared at him. "All right. I can and will do that. I never...I guess I thought with them here, I was safe, but I guess not. He was paying them off, wasn't he? To perhaps look the other way?"

"Yes, that would be correct." Raven sat there for several seconds with her eyes closed. "I can give you a list of the ones that you should have with you at all times. And a list of those that need to be thoroughly investigated."

Dinner was a nice affair. And before they left for home, Raven gave him the lists as well as a number of things that he needed to take care of. One of them was the little room downstairs. He hadn't known of it until then, he told her, but it would be gone, as well as the way to get in and out of there. Kirk was going to do well, they all thought. And Raven promised him that she'd keep an eye out for other things that he could do to make himself safe.

They didn't make the play that he'd wanted to see. Nor did they get to do much in the way of sightseeing. But Vance could live with that. He was happy with the way things had turned out and knew that as soon as he was in his new job, he was going to never think about the Army and what he'd done again.

Yeah, he thought to himself, and I'll not have nightmares either when my children start to date. Especially his daughters. Laughing, he realized that he was looking forward to the rest of his long life much more than he had before.

Chapter 11

Gavin stood up when the judge entered the room. He was thrilled to be here, in this room. His family was here too, and that made what was going on today much more important to him. Just yesterday he'd graduated from college, and today he was making his first court appearance. But it wasn't for anything major. Just something that he thought should have happened a very long time ago.

"This is an odd one, even for your family, Mr. McCade." He smiled; Gavin loved hearing his full name said to him. "You're here to represent your grandmother? What has she done now? And while we're on the subject, you do know that you're going to have to put someone else's name on the court documents. You must be at least twenty-one to come in here as an attorney."

"Yes, sir, I know, but Grandma insisted that I do this for her." Marcum nodded. "May I continue? That way Grandma

165

can go out sooner and get into more trouble before dinner time."

Grandma huffed. Gavin had to cover his mouth when he started to laugh. His grandma had made it her life's work, he thought, to cause trouble wherever she could. It was never dangerous trouble, or even, for the most part, against the law. But she did manage to make some sort of trouble where she had to be arrested.

"Well, Your Honor, as you know there are some sidewalks that are less than perfect. Wheelchairs have trouble riding over them, and at times people to go into the grass to get around. And that poses its own set of troubles." The judge nodded and said he'd seen the sidewalks. "Yes, sir. Several of them are in front of your house. Which brings me to my grandma. She has been after the city to come in and not just fix the sidewalks, but also to make sure that they're everywhere that people want to go. But they're not—the city workers aren't doing anything to them. And since my Uncle Vance has left town for a while, it's been harder and harder to get the workers to do much of anything. Just last week, the trash wasn't picked up for an entire day."

"Yes, I'm aware of that as well. I was told it was because of a scheduling issue." He asked if he could give him a report. "Come on now, we're not going to be all formal at this point, are we Gavin? Just tell me."

"There were ample people to work the streets, sir, but none of them wanted to go out in the heat to do their job. I have it on good authority that they sat in the offices all day, playing cards and drinking." He asked how he knew this.

166

"They neglected to turn off the cameras, and I have a copy of those recordings as well."

Marcum looked over the schedule as well as the report that he'd written on the men. "So you're going to tell me that these two things are related? Or that the same men were assigned this job and for the same reason didn't do it."

"Pretty much that's it, sir." The judge, Marcum McCade, one of his distant uncles from way back, asked for a computer to play the disc on. "There are two days on there, sir. The day that my grandma thought the sidewalks were going to be worked on, as well as the trash day. They did pick the trash up, but they're now a day and a half behind and going to be more so, and the animals will start going through it."

"The sidewalk project was supposed to take a month, correct?" Gavin told him it was to have begun work by now and been finished three days ago. "Nothing has been done to any of them?"

"It's why I was over there. Hoping that someone would take notice that they're a lazy bunch of people and need their butts kicked." Grandma stood up and spoke to Marcum like she had when she'd been at his house a few weeks ago for dinner. "I told you when the project was approved that there needed to be a timeline on this. And look at it now. Six weeks and nothing is done. I need those walks fixed up so that I don't have to trip up. You wouldn't want me to break one of my old hips, now would you?"

He didn't even try to have Grandma be quiet. Firstly, it would do him no good. She was on a roll. And secondly, she was right. It had taken her being out there and getting into

167

trouble to get someone to notice. Gavin just wished she'd tell him first when she was going to do something like this. Maybe he could avoid having to bail her out all the time.

He looked back at his parents when the baby made a noise. His baby sister, Alisha Grace, Allie as they called her, was almost one now, and he loved her as much as he ever thought he would. She was just the most adorable little girl he'd ever seen, and Gavin would do anything for her. And he was sure she knew it too.

Grady and his wife had a little boy, a little younger than his sister Allie. Allie and Bailey were a lot of fun to hang around with, and Gavin would watch them whenever he could. He didn't even mind changing dirty diapers. He just loved being with them.

While Marcum looked at the recordings, Gavin thought of his family. In the almost two years now since they'd moved here, things had turned out very well. The town was prospering, the people in it were happy, and he'd never seen his family, all of them, this thrilled about life as they seemed to be now. Even Grandma, with all her mischief, seemed to be having the best time of all of them.

Uncle Kenton and his wife were going to have their baby any day now. And he'd been going around town acting like he'd invented having children. Everyone loved the man, and he had set up his practice in town with a waiting list of people that wanted to come see him. Aunt Emma had even been baking, though not on the scale she'd been baking at home. Wedding cakes, it seemed, was what she did best.

Dad was working hard on his craft. That's what he called

it, his craft. Some of his paintings were in the White House now. He'd been asked to paint the president, and had done it very well. It was awesome to think that his dad had works of art in such a wonderful place. His mom was working for Just Perfect now, finding things, items that could be used on sets of television shows and stuff. Gavin was so proud of her that he could nearly bust. The first time he'd gone to see a movie her things were in, he'd not even paid any attention to the story, just waited for the credits where her name was blazing across the big screen as a coordinator of the sets. Well, it wasn't really blazing, but he'd found it easily enough.

Uncle Grady didn't work on computers much anymore. He was better at setting up the cameras and such around town. He'd put in cameras to catch someone running lights, to find people that might be on the run, as well as working with some people that weren't even in the same country. They had him doing it, just to make sure they had the best there was. Harper was the best potter he had ever known, not that he knew all that many. And her things, too, were in the White House on display.

Uncle Dalton was cooking at the shelter. Gavin thought that of all his uncles, he enjoyed his job the most. He also ran the place and made sure that the people there had what they needed. But he only took credit for filling their bellies. He was a good man and a cop forever, Gavin thought. Gabe worked with him. She made sure that everyone was healthy and that the meals they were eating from Uncle Dalton were healthy too. Aunt Gabe had been called on to help out Uncle Kenton once in a while, and she had a blast delivering babies.

169

Lewis had a nice restaurant now. It wasn't nearly as large as Dragon's Lair had been, but it served up a lot of nice meals that he was proud of. It was only open on weekends. The rest of the time he helped Aunt Emma with her cakes, and had been known to make a few pies for dinner too.

Aunt Raven worked at getting gardens in areas opened and ready for planting. Not just for herbs, though she had a lot of them, but also gardens for those who wanted to grow a veggie or two. That was a big thing with the high school kids; being able to grow something to have at dinner was something that even he enjoyed.

"Mr. McCade?" Gavin looked at Judge Marcum and told him he was sorry. "That's all right. I can see here that you've given me a list of the names, as well as the duties that they should have been taking care of. Is this right? I mean, Vance and his wife have only been gone a few weeks."

"Yes, sir, it's correct. I've worked hard at trying to find the dates on the projects as well. Dates they were started and when they should have been completed. Some of those that I found were before my uncle took over as mayor. I'm sure that he wasn't made aware of them, so they'd not be in more trouble from him. So far, as you can see, only one project has been completed, and I think that was only because it benefited them. The new lunch room project at the maintenance shop is done and over budget, believe it or not."

"With all this information, yes, I can believe it." He searched the paperwork more and then set it down. "I don't suppose I can talk you into helping me with more projects, can I? Having a man like you on my side, it would go a long way in getting things completed on time and under budget, I'm betting."

"I'm only seventeen, sir." Grandma snorted at the same time Marcum did. "Well, I am. I just turned seventeen, and while I have fun at this, Grandma gets into too much trouble for me to be tied up at something else. She needs me as much as I do her."

"I'm thinking that with your mom's permission, we can work something out. And if you and I can get on these with Vance's help, your grandma would be in less trouble. At least we can hope for that." Gavin told him if he could convince his mom, then he was all right with it too. "Good. I'll talk to her tonight then."

Marcum let Grandma go on the promise that she gave him a week to get a new crew in and working on the sidewalks. Before he allowed her to go, however, he asked her what she was working on next. Grandma told him that she'd contact him when she was ready to tell him.

"You know that you have my permission, don't you?" Gavin hugged his little sister to him and she squealed in delight. Mom kissed him on the cheek as she continued. "Was there a reason you didn't tell him yes?"

"I'm not sure that I want to be the bad guy. And I will be, won't I?" She told him he could handle it. "Yeah, I know that, but I'm worried. These guys aren't very nice. And they already have it out for Uncle Vance."

"Vance is on his way home with Micky. You can know now, but he left so that this would all come to a head." Gavin asked Dad why he'd not told him. "He wanted to see if you could handle it. And I told him what you'd done and what you were able to find out. He's very proud of you. In fact, he said that you found a few things he'd not been aware of. Go tell Marcum you'll help him. You know you want to."

Gavin did too. It was fun doing research on things. And the more he dug into things, the more he seemed to learn. To him, learning was everything. He moved back to the door that led to the offices of the judge and knocked.

When the door opened, he smiled at Marcum, who stood there no longer in his robes but shorts and a college T-shirt. He even had on flip flops. In one hand he had a cold cola, and a cookie was hanging out of his mouth. Gavin loved this man.

"You're going to work for me?" Gavin nodded and went into his office. "Good. But we're going to pay you. You can't do this sort of work without a check. I know you have money, but to balance the books, I have to make sure that you're paid."

"Can I donate the money?" He said whatever he did with it was fine by him. "Okay. I can help with a few other projects I have in mind. Did you know that there are no after school programs for the little kids?"

Marcum laughed. "I tell you, kid, if I didn't know for a fact that you weren't blood related to my dad, I'd swear the two of you were twins in the way that you think about things. I tell you this all the time, young man, but I'm so glad that you're a part of this family."

"Me too." They talked about what projects he wanted to get started on and the fact that Vance was coming home. After a couple of hours, he left for home to sit his sister for the evening. Gavin loved his new life.

~~~

Vance didn't make a sound as he walked into the big maintenance building. It was a great building—old, but up to date on everything to make the workers comfortable. Maybe too comfortable. Today was going to be the most fun he'd had as mayor, and he was glad someone had finally taken notice of the workers in town.

"He's going to cause us some trouble, that kid is. What's he got against us? It's not like he has anything to do with the jobs we've put under the rugs." Vance paused before entering the room where the workers met every morning. He might find out about more than just the projects that were undone. "Last week, when we were supposed to be working on the broken line in the street? That kid came right over and asked what we were doing. Like he would know if we told him."

"He probably does know. He's pretty smart. You talking about the day that we had the cookout under the streets? Man, that was a blast, and so much cooler than behind one of our houses. That was a brilliant idea you had, Blue, to fake a break so we could go down there and not be bothered." Vance pulled out his phone and made notes about what they were saying. Then he asked his brother Grady to turn the cameras on if they were off.

Got it. Hey, did you know that all the cameras are off in that building? It looks like someone tripped a circuit. I can fix that too. Dumbasses. Okay, Vance, we're rolling. He asked him if there was audio. *Yes. However, I don't think they're aware of it. I put that in for free when I wired the room up.*

173

I owe you. Is there a way that they can think they turned them off – the cameras, I mean – yet they still run? He said he'd have to put in other cameras, but he could do that. *I'll pay for it. I might not need it after today, but I'll pay for it being done. This has been going on long enough.*

Grady told him he'd do it for him, and Vance listened more to the men complain about Gavin. The kid had made some enemies, but not anything that they couldn't handle if they came after him. Actually, Vance was hoping they would. He was just in that sort of mood.

Vance knew the kid would look into things, and having Mom helping him out by getting into trouble again was perfect. Vance loved being the mayor of this little burg, but he also needed to be taken seriously. The men in the other room hadn't done that for a very long time. Today was going to make them pay attention to a lot of new rules. One of which was, either do the work in a reasonable timeframe or he'd find someone that would.

Most of the people in the room were going to be fired. The crew that was out working and did so every day would be spared. They might have done the jobs had they known about them, but time would tell. He was sick and tired of paying for things not being done.

Moving around the doorway, just inside the room, he watched them to see if anyone would notice. There were several beer cans on the table that were still frosty with cold. The air conditioning in the room was set on about sixty degrees; there was a nice chill in the place. Also, he saw several boxes of pizza, as well as two large boxes that had the bakery name on them. When he was finally noticed, he waved at the man.

"He's here."

The men scrambled to clean up the mess. Beer cans were tossed in the general direction of the trash can, which was overflowing with more of the same. Vance just stood there, letting them fall all over themselves as they blamed each other for the mess as well as sitting around.

"We were just discussing some of the projects that you put out for us." Vance said nothing as he made his way into the room. "There are a lot of them out there. We were just deciding on which one was the most important."

"Were you? It sounded to me like you were making plans to go after my nephew for having the judge, whom I left in charge while I was away, make you get to work. Had you done the job as you should have in the first place, you'd not be in hot water. Or fired." They looked at each other, then laughed. "You think it's funny that you might be fired?"

"You can't fire us. We're the only people you got to do these jobs." Vance pointed out that they weren't doing the jobs at all. "Yeah, we'll get around to them. But right now, it's like ninety degrees out there, and it's better to sit in here rather than get heat stroke. It's dangerous for us to be working."

"Dangerous, huh? And how about the men that are out there now? Doing the job as best they can without supervision or help? What do you think they'll think about you sitting in here, having a beer and some pizza? I'd think they'd be pissed. I know that I am." The first man, Conley was on his name badge, puffed out his chest and said once again how he needed them. "No. I don't. As a matter of fact, you have a choice. And I will require you to answer me honestly. Do you want to do the job that you're paid to do or not?"

They'd not be able to lie to him. He was powerful enough, thanks to Caelin, that no one would ever lie to him. But these men, he'd come to realize, were very stupid, and compulsion didn't work as well on them.

"I don't fucking want to work for some outsider." Vance nodded and asked if there was anyone else that felt that way. "What do you care if we do the work or not?" Conley asked him.

"Because the town pays me to make you do the job." Conley said he wasn't given a big house nor a car to ride around in. "Good point. And you're fired. As are the rest of you. You have one hour to clean out your crap. Make sure you don't take anything that belongs here, and the police will escort you off the property."

Two hours later he had a new crew with the ones that had stayed, as well as a list of work that he wanted done as soon as possible. They were all told that there would be no slacking anymore, and if caught, not only would they lose their jobs, but their pensions as well. Vance left with a heavy heart. Some of those people had families.

You can't take on the world, Vance. He smiled when Micky spoke to him. *I have an idea. You come home, take Caelin for a little while, and I'll take a nap. He's been on the go since you left us this morning. Why did I ever want him to learn to walk?*

Because you don't want to have to carry him anymore. He'd weighed twenty-two pounds at his last doctor's visit. Kenton said he was healthy and happy, and not the least bit

176

overweight. *At one and a half, we have a bruiser for a son and you love it. But I have to stop by the office for a little while. Bring him there and I'm sure there are any number of things he can get into with me. Also, he's charmed all of them into having treats for him at their desks.*

Micky laughed and said she'd do it. *He's been on fire all day. I think he missed home while we were gone. And Gavin came by and the two of them took a walk before he had to go to work. I'm so glad that you got him that job. He's feeling pretty good about himself.*

Vance had noticed that Gavin was feeling a little down. He had graduated from college a while back, and now he was working on another degree. Having him sit with Caelin seemed to be the highlight of the kid's week. Vance thought he needed a girlfriend. He didn't have much in the way of friends. Even Mom had pointed that out.

Going to his office, he was greeted not only by Micky and his son, but the elder Caelin was there as well. He was holding his son, laughing at the way he just jabbered about everything. Waiting until Micky went home to take her much needed nap, he asked the man what was up.

"Nothing. Not much anyway. I'm glad that you're back." He told him what he'd done since he'd returned. "You don't have to report to me, Vance. I know that you're working to get us a nicer place to live. Besides, Marcum told me all about it. I would have loved to have seen their faces."

"What's going on? I know you well enough to know that there is something. You just don't pop into this office without something on your plate. You know that you can depend on

177

any of us to help." Caelin nodded. "Tell me before I have to shake it out of you."

"I want to leave here." Vance didn't have a smart assed comment to reply back to him. "See, you wanted it right now, when I was willing to ease into it. My wife and I want to travel a little bit. A few years. We've seen the world, she and I, but so much has changed since we've been about that she and I would love to go on a trip."

"You should." Caelin cocked a brow at him. "I'm not saying that I want you to leave right now, but the two of you deserve to get away. But you will return, won't you?"

"I'm not sure at this point." Vance could understand that too. Caelin had lived here for decades, watching over things for them. "We're tired. Not to the point where we want to curl into a ball and let the world go on around us, but we do want to get away. Someplace that no one knows what we are or who we are. It's something that has been on our mind of late since you've done such a good job here."

"I've done a shitty job if that means you want to leave us." They both laughed. "You're telling me this first, why? I'm not in charge any more than Conley was at the office building today. Why me?"

"I want to leave the town in good hands. You're the mayor, and I think that you've exceeded my expectations for it. You've not only taken care of the job you were assigned to, but there are several new businesses going in with the residents. We also have a new playground for the school, as well as three new buses for students. You've made sure that there is ample funding for the teachers to have what they

178

need when they need it. That one slipped by me." Vance told him it was easy to miss. "No, you found it right away that the teachers were using some of their own money to put supplies in their rooms. I know that they thanked you for that several times over."

"Yes. We have been thanked plenty. But that can't be the reason you came to me, is it? I know that Kenton has done a good job as king of the dragons. And they're coming back, too. Just the other day he told me that you have six new hatchlings due to come into the world any day now." Caelin nodded with a smile. "What about Lewis? He can—"

"Say 'Yes, Caelin, I'll do what you need for me to do so you can go on a vacation'." Vance repeated it back to him. "I know that leaving you in charge, you'll gladly ask for help when you need it. Kenton wouldn't. He'd think that since I asked him to keep the town from going to pot, he'd need to devote every second of every minute to it. The rest of them would as well."

He was right. When Kenton had been asked to see that the breeding dragons had enough space to move around, he'd nearly gotten himself buried under the mountain by setting charges to blow larger caves in the place. Had Vance not been walking in the woods with Micky, Kenton might well have brought the entire mountain down on top of them. As it was, they had to make sure that someone came in to get the charges out.

"So you'll do it? You'll take over the running of the town for me?" Vance didn't want to, because to do so would mean that Caelin would leave. And he enjoyed the man's company too much for that to happen. "What if I told you that I'd contact you weekly, to just talk about anything you wish?"

"You're making this very difficult for me." Caelin told him that was the plan. "I see. All right then. You go on your trip and I'll take care of things here. But I warn you, the first time I don't hear from you, I'm going to find you and bring you back here. I love you, Caelin."

"And I you, Vance. You were the most difficult of all the brothers to find someone for. I can tell you that now. She had to be strong willed, as you are. Smart, because you'd never be attracted to someone that wasn't. And she had to have the heart to love you." He asked why that was so hard, finding someone to have a heart to love him. "Because when I first found you, you were broken. I was worried that you might not be fixable. You had a hard life, my young friend, and in doing so, your heart was closed off to anyone new. Micky, while older than you, had much the same kind of life as you. But she was softer, in many ways, for you."

Vance was still in his office, rocking his exhausted son, when Micky came to join him. Handing her the little man, he kissed them both then held them in his arms. Vance knew how blessed he was; he thanked his lucky stars every day that he'd been chosen for her. Vance also knew, for as long as he lived, the dragons would have a very special meaning for him.

Chapter 12

Caelin lay beside his lovely wife and held her in his arms. They were complete, he thought. They had all that they could ever want, their children had children of their own, and the dragons were cared for. The McCades, his generation of them, as he called them, had gone well beyond what he had ever expected of them.

"He will care for the town for us?" Caelin told her that he would. "And what did he demand of you as compensation? I know that he did. He will not want much, but something from you."

"He wants me to talk to him once a week, about nothing at all. He said that he loved me as well." She asked him if he thought that odd. "No. Perhaps from another person that I have no trust in, but I know that Vance does love me without any strings attached to it. He is a good man."

"Of course he is. I've told the children, and they're going

to pass it on to the others. When can we leave?" She was so excited that he didn't want to tell her to wait. "I can have us booked on the first leg of our journey by the morning if you allow me to."

"I could never deny you a thing, my love. You book us, and we'll leave as soon as it is light enough for us to see." She clapped her hands and went to the office. He could hear her talking to someone, and decided to go to the den and have a nice rest. He hadn't aged in a very long time, but that didn't mean that he didn't tire easily.

Caelin would love to be here all the time. And what he'd told Vance was only partly true. They did want to get away, to see the world once again. But he and his wife were going to never return. They were going to find them a nice beach, call the faeries to them, and be put to rest. Forever. Caelin closed his eyes and saw his mother there, dressed in her finest gown and looking as fresh and wonderful as she had all those years ago when he'd left her at the castle.

"You wish to leave before I can come back to you?" He told her that he was tired. That he'd waited for someone to come along to take over longer than most had. "Yes, you have. As have I. I am.... It has occurred to me that I don't think I have it in me to be a part of this family either. I will pass on my magic, and then leave as well. I was wondering all this time how to tell you."

"You and I, we have been apart for many years, Mother. Too many for us to be able to take up where we left off. I have seen you, a great many times, but was never able to speak to you, or to touch you as I wished." She said that it saddened her to think how much she had missed. "We both have. But you've been around here of late, haven't you? Seeing to the children of mine. Visiting where you could. I'm glad that you have, but it makes me miss you all the more."

"Yes, myself as well. I miss you." He watched her move around in his dream-like state, and when she paused, he could see the large chair that had been a part of the castle. "Do you ever wonder what might have been had Butler not come into my life? I'd still want to have you there with me, but perhaps you'd be different as well. I made a mistake taking him to my castle. I should have done more to keep him out of my life."

"Had you done that, Mother, you know that someone else would have come along and taken it from you. The time had been that way. And without the help of Warrior, there is no telling what might have happened to any of us. Including Warrior." He noticed the faraway look in her eyes, the one that his own wife had only recently pointed out to him. "You love him, don't you, Mother?"

"Warrior? Yes. I think I always have. To be free to love him as I want, it would be a great gift, but one that I cannot hope to have." She stood up and moved to the large throne that he'd played on as a small boy. "When he helped me birth you, I saw what a man was really like. A man that gave more than he would ever be able to receive. But even before that, he owned my heart. And now he shares it only with you."

"I'm sorry." She waved him off, but he thought of all that she had suffered so that others might have more. "You can visit us when we leave here."

"Nay, you know that I cannot. I am now bound here

because the McCades have come at last." She smiled then, brilliantly. "You have so many children and grandchildren that I don't think I could have imagined it when you were but a babe. I love to see them, playing and having fun. How I wish that I could have seen you do the things they are doing."

"I was a boring child, Mother. I only worked hard so that I could free you and Warrior." She looked sad again, and he thought of something that would cheer her up. "You should be with Alisha sometimes. She gets into more trouble than most of the smaller children here. I swear to you, she is like one of the dragons that gets into mischief all the time."

"I was in the courtroom this morn. She is having the time of her life, I think. And she drags young Gavin with her everywhere just to make him have fun too. He is much too serious, I think, for one so young." He agreed with her. "I must go soon. Please tell me when you are to go. I would wish to see you once more."

"We hope to leave in the morning, but I will let you know. I think there might be a delay or two with things." He was going to make sure of it. Caelin had a plan. "You will always have a place here, Mother. And the faeries, they know what to do if you wish to leave."

"Yes, I've spoken to them as well." She started to fade a little, but came back for a moment longer. "I love you, Caelin, my son. And I will love you forever and a day."

When she left him there, he woke, his mind still centered on the conversation and what he must do now. Calling to the magical creatures all over the land, he was glad when they answered him with their promise of help. He was going to make his mother happy if it was the last thing that he did. When he had all that he could from the lands, he called to Raven and Micky. They would be the final touch that he'd need.

I need for you to meet me at the caves of the castle. Both said they'd be there. *Bring your animals, please, and I will need the dragons too. All that you have with you.*

They were all there when he arrived at the caves. He was surprised to see all the McCades, but knew that he shouldn't have been. They were a family that helped when they could, and this time was no different.

Caelin called for Warrior to come to him. The dragon looked like he had all those many decades ago. He was a brilliant blue, his body long and hard with armor that was his to use. The tail that he used in battle was spiked with hard blades, his face covered in scars, as well as a face mask that took care of the worst of the blows he might have had.

The armor at his chest carried the seal of the family; the large dragon was Warrior, his wings spread out and his fire blowing hotly from his nose. There were none more powerful than the dragon in front of him, and there never would be. Not unless he found him a mate, and that just wasn't possible. Not yet, at any rate.

"You love my mother?" The warrior bowed low before him, his body still high enough that you could see the top of the mountain from it. When he said that he did, and had forever, Caelin asked if she loved him as well.

"Yes, my lord. We have loved each other well before you were birthed, and since then for all eternity. She has my heart in her hand to do with as she pleases."

Caelin looked at the people there with him. All the magic that he could summon would not have been enough without all of them there.

The dragons left the bodies of their hosts. Roderick and Lyna, even as small as they were, they were as powerful as any of the other dragons on the land. There were others there as well, their offspring, as well as visiting dragons.

Vance drew his sword and the air hummed with the power of it. He said a few words, and just behind him stood his own dragon, dark in color, her body strong and true. With a request from Vance, the entire mountain and all the creatures on it would be dead. A single breath from her and there would be nothing left.

Micky called her own dragon. To Vance's blue female, her dragon was light. He was just as powerful, but his magic wasn't his breath, but water. He was a dragon that would be the perfect foil for a fire dragon. It was why he'd matched them together.

Caelin only nodded once, and when he did, he was nearly knocked over with the amount of freely given magic to use. The queen of faeries came as well, then the queen of the brownies. The magic would be just what he needed, and he turned to Warrior.

"Had you a name, what would you call yourself?" He looked up from his position on the ground, but laid his head back and asked what he meant. "A name. What is it you'd like to be called should you be a man?"

"I was called many names, my lord. But there is only one

186

name that I should like to be called; it would be McCade." Caelin looked at the men that had brought them so much, and each of them nodded. "I'm sorry to question you, my lord, but what are you about?"

"I will give the magic to you and my mother. What it will do with the two of you, I know not." His mother came then, to stand next to her dragon. "This magic is given freely. It will be yours for the taking. To be used to make you lovers. To give you the chance that you never had to be together. I, Caelin of the McCade family, give this and all that I have to bring the two people I love most in this world happiness."

He felt the power of the magic explode around him. There was so much of it that what wasn't used by the couple before him would make the earth very fertile for the next several hundred years. The trees would give so much fruit that there would be much canning and making of jellies. The lake beyond would have so many fish in it that he knew the women and men of the town would be drying and smoking them well into winter. All the magic that surrounded his mother and the dragon swirled around them. Then they disappeared.

Caelin fell to the ground. He wasn't just exhausted, but it felt as if every part of him had been drained. When he felt the small touch of someone behind him, he smiled up at Micky when his strength was returned, and he felt better than he had in a while. Standing up with the help of Vance, he noticed a difference in them immediately.

"You've changed." Vance laughed. "What is it? Something has changed you. The magic? Was that it?"

"No, this happened before you left today. And when I

talked to Micky a bit later, she got it too." Their hair was now longer, and streaked with an inch-wide strip of silver. Not white or gray, but a very shiny silver. It suited them both. "Not only that, but I do believe that our dragons to call are larger. They certainly are on our bodies."

He had noticed that they were larger in a vague sort of way, but hadn't been paying attention. Caelin was more focused on his task and what it would mean for the two people that had brought him into this world.

"What will happen to them?" Caelin told Alisha that he hoped that Warrior would be a man, so that he might be with his mother for all time. "But you don't know for sure. What could happen to them?"

"They could be just as they are now. Or Mother will become a part of him. I gave them the magic to do with as they wished. There was more than enough for Warrior to become a man. I hope that, of all things, is what happens."

He went home to finish his packing. Caelin should have known that his wife would not only have it finished, but would have them booked on the first flight out. He knew not where they were going but was happy because she was. And when they left just as the sun was coming up over the mountain, he still had no idea what Warrior would look like.

"They'll be happy, no matter what you have done for them." He told her that he knew that, but he wished to have seen her once again. "We will return, if only to see her once more."

"I don't know, love. If we return, we might not want to leave again. And you and I need to start anew. Or to sleep."

188

She kissed him on the mouth and he smiled. "What was that for, may I ask?"

"I love you. You can be very silly at times, but I do love you. Now, think of all that we're about to embark on, and tell me what you think of a ship. We'll be on one for a month, traveling around the world." Caelin told her that was what he wanted to do, see the world with her. "And you shall. But I also wish to send home gifts to be hidden away for Christmas. I have spoken to Alisha, and she said she'd do it for us. Oh, Caelin, I'm so excited that I could burst wide open."

The first leg of their journey was going to be a long one. The flight was taking them to a remote place, she'd told him, and from there, they'd board a ship. Caelin was glad for it, but he still thought of his mother. He only hoped that she'd be happy with Warrior being her man now.

~~~

Micky dug the small plant out of the dirt and laid it gently in the basket she had. There were several other plants in her basket, but none as treasured as this one. Dragon's tail was a prize that she never thought she'd find in these woods. Standing up, she looked around for more of the flowering plant, and saw a few others just beyond her. Walking there, careful of the other plants, she kept an eye out for anyone coming around.

For the last several days she'd had a feeling that there were others in the woods when she was out. Nothing that would harm her, at least she didn't think so, but she knew as surely as she was there that someone was around. Just as she bent to dig out another of the plants, she felt her dragon stir

189

and she paused in what she was doing.

The small child came around the tall oak and stared at her. Micky wasn't going to assume that it was a child, and not a child in sheep's clothing. There still wasn't the feeling of being harmed, but she wasn't going to take any chances. People, she knew, would do anything if they wanted.

The child came out from behind the tree and stared hard at her.

"Are you lost?" The child just shook its head. From where she sat, Micky couldn't tell if it was a male child or female. "What's your name, child?"

"Pena." She nodded and asked her if she was hungry. "I am, but I have to find my own food. I'm not to take things from strangers."

"Are you alone, Pena? Do you have your parents nearby, or perhaps a brother or sister?" She said that her parents were dead, but she had a little sister. "Where is she? Is she hungry too?"

"I killed them." The dragon at her waist seemed to curl tighter around her. "They were hurting us. The teacher said that don't supposed to happen."

"How were they hurting you?" She pointed to her chest, then between her legs. "Who touched you there?"

"Do you have food on you?" She didn't, but that didn't mean she couldn't make some for the little girl. "I'm very hungry. And so is my sister."

"You bring me your sister, and I'll feed you both." She looked back behind her and Micky started digging at the plants again. "Or you could just go and find your own food for the two of you."

"She's little. My sister, her name is Kerrie. She won't be easy to feed." She asked her why not. "I don't have no milk for her."

So, the child was young. "Go and get her, bring her to me, and we'll make sure that you're both safe and fed."

Pena didn't seem to want to leave her. Whether she thought that Micky would leave without the promised food or she was afraid to get her sister, Micky wasn't sure. But she'd not leave them. No matter what.

She told the child that she wanted to dig for a little while longer. Micky had all that she dared take from the dragon's tail, but she'd find herself more things to take home. When Pena left her, she called to Raven; the witch would know what to do. When she appeared beside her with a basket full of plants and a small knife, she asked her if she'd been looking too.

"No, but I thought if it looked like we were together, then she'd not bolt. I can feel her; she is hungry, and the baby, another little girl, is about starved. We'll have to find a wet nurse for her." Micky told her what Pena had said. "Yes, she's been abused. The baby hasn't been, but it was close. Pena killed them both by poison. She knows her plants too."

They moved around the ground, not really pulling anything more but talking about the things that they'd found. When Pena returned, she had a baby bundled in her arms, but she didn't come any closer. Micky was afraid they'd both starve to death if she didn't do something now.

"This is my sister, Raven. Raven, this is Pena and Kerrie.

I was going to take them to my house and feed them a fine feast." Raven asked if she could see the baby, but Pena backed up. "You will not leave here again. You'll come to me."

She fought her, so hard that her nose bled from it, but finally, in the end, Raven took the baby and Micky held onto Pena. They were both unwell. Raven took the quickest route home, magic. Micky couldn't do that, not with a sick child in her arms. Their magic was different, and while she could do a lot of the things that Raven could, transporting two people was something that only Raven could do. When she returned, saying that she'd found someone to feed the child, she asked if Pena would come with her to see her sister.

"She's gonna be filled up with milk? I don't have none. I tried, but I don't have none." Micky asked her how old she was. "I'll be seven in the winter. My momma said that I was as cold as the day she birthed me. And she didn't like Kerrie none either."

"Well, I'm glad that you came to us." When they got to the house, Micky assured her that she'd be welcome. She had contacted Vance to let him know what was going on, and he was on the porch when they came up the steps. "Vance is my husband. He's been making sure that the town is run right."

"Hello." Pena hid behind her and didn't go anywhere near Vance. "I have some cookies for you, should you like them. My sister and brother cook all the time, and they just dropped off some of the best ones I've ever eaten. I can share them with you if you'd like."

"I've never had a cookie before." Pena moved around Micky, but didn't go any further toward Vance than to take a cookie from his outstretched hand. When she broke it in half, putting part of it into her dirty dress pocket, Micky felt her heart tear up. The child was starving, and would save some of this for later.

Taking her into the house, Raven took Pena to see her sister. One of the women in the town had just recently had a baby, and had been more than happy to help out. The baby was weak, but with a little magic from Micky, she ate until her belly was full. Pena sat very still on the chair when a burger and fries were set in front of her.

"Now, I know that you're thinking we'd hurt you," Vance took a fry and put the whole thing in his mouth as he cut her burger in half. "We'd never do that. You know who we are too, don't you?"

"The McCades." Vance nodded and took a bite of her burger. "You won't poison me, will you? I had to do it. They were hurting me, and they were gonna hurt my little sister. She's hard to care for, but she's my sister."

"I know that. I have a son here; did you know that?" She said that she'd not heard that. "His name is Caelin. I have to tell you something, I think he'd love to have a big sister like you. Would you like that?"

Pena eyed Vance hard, like she was studying him for something that he might want from her. Vance for the most part ignored her, eating his own burger and fries as he got them all a glass of tea. When she finally took one of the halves of the burger off the plate and started eating it, Vance cautioned her to eat slowly so she'd not be sick.

"It's been a while since you had any food, so if you eat too

193

fast, your belly will be upset and make it all come back up. So take your time. There are plenty of cookies to be had." Pena ate slowly then, taking a small bite and chewing it fully before swallowing. "See, you're doing just fine."

Micky watched the two of them eat. Vance did most of the talking, telling her about their son and the house that she was in. And casually, he asked about her parents between other things. Pena answered him, telling him not only what had happened, but where the bodies were.

"My dad, he was nasty to me. I know that he's not supposed to touch me like that." Vance asked her how many times he'd done it. "All the time. But momma, she said that I should just shut my trap and let him. It'd be over soon."

"I'm glad that you knew it wasn't right. But to kill them, that's sort of sad, don't you think? I mean, maybe they could have gotten some help." Pena shook her head. "You don't think so?"

"I told him I weren't gonna do it no more. That it hurts me when I have to pee and stuff. But he slapped me all over." She stood up and lifted her shirt. The marks on her small body were terrifying. "I hurt real bad after that, and he went after Kerrie. She's just a baby, and I had to keep him off her. Momma, she was real mad on account 'a she said she'd have to take my place. Momma said it was better for me than her. That ain't right."

"No, it's not right at all." Vance looked at Micky, then back at the little girl as he spoke softly to her. "I'm going to get my big brother Kenton. He's a doctor, and I want him to have a look at your sores. You can trust him not to hurt you.

194

He's a very nice man with children of his own."

"I need to see to my sister. She's gonna need me too." Vance told her that Kenton would want to examine her as well, just to make sure that she didn't have a cold. "I tried real hard not to let her get a chill. But we'd been outside for a long time."

"Do you know how long you've been outside, Pena?" She said she didn't, but Micky could see that she was exhausted. She was having a hard time keeping her eyes open. "How about you go with Micky here, and I'll go and get my brother. While you're getting a bath, I can have him look at your sister."

"He'd better not hurt her. I'm little, but I'm mean too." Vance said that he could see that about her, but no one would hurt them again. When Micky was taking her to the bathroom to have a bath, she asked her what her last name was. "I'm a Stevenson, but that ain't my dad's last name. His is Walter. My sister was born this year, but I don't remember when. I'm sure tired. Can I take me a nap first, please?"

"I think you'd sleep much better all cleaned up. And one of my friends is going to bring you a pretty gown to put on to sleep in. You don't want to get it dirty, do you?" Pena said she didn't, but yawned again. "Let's hurry up so you can rest."

Micky was heartbroken by the time she'd tucked Pena into a bed. Sobbing while standing outside her bedroom, she cried quietly against Vance's chest as he wrapped her into his arms. He never said a word to her — she wasn't sure what he could say to her that she'd hear right now — but just having him hold her, that was enough for now.

"Kenton said he'd examine her while she's asleep. He's

195

going to give her a little something to put her under more. He thinks that if what she says is true, she'll stress out when he tries to touch her." She nodded and looked up at him. "The baby is all right. Undernourished, but he said a few more meals and she should be better. He wants us to keep up with having her nursed; it'll make her stronger."

"She's so hurt, Vance. Like someone took a whip to her little body. And the way she talks about killing them, it's as if she felt that she'd done the right thing." Vance said that she probably had. "I know that, but I worry that it'll come back on her someday, what she's done to her parents."

"We'll be here for her. I've asked my family if they'd help us with the search for the bodies." She told him the last names and he said that would help. "I'm not sure what we'll find there, but you should stay here with her. Pena might have nightmares before this is all over. If she's asleep, I'll call Kenton up."

The examination showed that she'd been sexually abused, and it had been over a long period of time. The child had a broken rib and her knee was badly bruised. Kenton was amazed that she'd been able to get around at all, much less care for a baby.

And he was angry. Micky had never seen Kenton so angry. He told her several times that he was sorry, for what she wasn't sure, but she hugged him when he seemed to lose the little control he had over himself.

"They did that to their own child." She said that she didn't understand it either. "I would have killed them myself if they were right here right now. I don't understand how anyone, especially a parent, could do that to a child."

"I don't either. But they're safe now, and we're going to take them." Kenton said that if they had any doubts about this, he'd take them as well. "I think we'll be fine with it. She's comfortable here, and she's already settled. But she'll need a good uncle, a bunch of them, and aunts to make sure that she knows that she's loved, as well as her sister."

"You know that we'll do that." She said that she did. "I'm going to talk to the rest of them. Let them know what we've found out here. They've gone to find the bodies, and Gabe is going to examine them for the region. I'm glad, and not happy that I can't do it. If they're alive, if I were there, they'd not be for long."

"I think that Vance feels the same way." They sat in the living room as Pena and her sister slept. She cuddled with Caelin while he slept, needing to hold onto him right now. Kenton said that he understood. That he wished he could do the same.

Handing him her son, she reached into the makeshift cradle of Kerrie and held her. The little girl was so pretty that Micky felt her heart hurt again for what these little girls had endured to live.

Chapter 13

Pena and Kerrie were in her bedroom. So much had changed in the last decade or so. Kerrie was going to be fifteen soon, and Pena had turned twenty-two three months ago. Life, she had figured out, had a way of just changing in a heartbeat, and for her and her little sister, it had turned out very well. Not all children that had been abused like them had had it so well.

"When is he getting here?" Pena laughed and said not until two-thirty. "I can't wait that long. I bet he's very handsome all dressed up in his suit."

"I've not seen him in one. He's always in jeans and a T-shirt when I see him." Kerrie nodded. "You and I, we have one thing to do today before this happens. Are you ready for it?"

"Yes, but I don't remember them at all. I'm glad, but I don't." Pena said that she remembered them well enough for the two of them. "I'm ready when you are."

Pena had promised herself that on this day, she'd go and see the graves of her parents. They'd been dead for the same fifteen years that she'd been safe and happy. The McCades had been more than good to her. They'd been the best parents that anyone could ever hope to have. And not only did she have her little sister Kerrie, but she had two brothers now, and three sisters.

Some of them had been like her — children that had been hurt. Not all of them sexually, as she had been, but hurt all the same. And since she'd come to age, as she called it, Pena had decided that she wanted to be there for them as much as Kenton and the others had been for her. So graduating at the age of fifteen, and with the support of so many people, she'd gone to college to become a counselor as well as a pediatrician. It was her life's dream to be the best she could, too.

They walked along the tree line. She knew that they weren't buried in a cemetery. The McCades had left them where they were as the house, the shack really, had been burned down around them. For a long time they told her that it was gone when they got there, but when she figured out they were dragons, she had reckoned out that they were the ones that had done it. To spare her, Mom had told her. Pena was grateful for that as well.

She hadn't been here before today. Pena had thought about it over the years, but never got up the nerve to do so until now. Her life was about to have another change in it, and she was happy to finally come here and talk to her parents.

Closure. She knew what the word meant now, and what

it meant to her. Today she was going to go and tell them what she thought of them, as well as how her life was going now. Today, Pena was marrying the man of her dreams.

The ground where the house had been was dark. Nothing would grow there, she'd been told. The dragons had burned the ground deep and destroyed all that would have ever grown where the house had once set. Anger had made them do this. Anger at what she and Kerrie had lived with, and what they'd done to her as a child.

"Why did they die?" No one had ever told Kerrie what had happened to their parents. They had decided well before she was old enough to think of such things that it would hurt her and Pena to have to explain the why of it. So she told them what everyone thought—that the house caught fire while they were sleeping, and they died. "Is that true, Pena? I mean, I hear you having bad dreams. They hurt you, didn't they?"

"Yes. They did." She was willing to leave it at that if Kerrie would. She looked at the ground and thought of what she'd practiced to say to them. "You know, I was going to tell them about what today meant to me. What I was going to do with my life, but I don't think I will."

"They wouldn't care." No, even alive, she doubted that they'd care. "I think that when I grow up, I want to come out here and plant a tree. I don't know if it'll grow up or not, but I'm going to do it."

"I think you should."

The sky darkened above them, but neither of them moved. Pena was sure she knew who was visiting them, and she smiled when the large dragons landed nearby. Kerrie squealed in delight, and Pena made her way to the big blue dragon and hugged him tightly.

"Warrior, how are you doing today? I would have thought you'd be home, watching over your hatchlings." He laughed and bumped his head gently to hers. "I love you too, you big softy. Are you and Prisane going to be at the wedding today?"

"We'd not miss it for the world." Prisane lay down on the grass and Kerrie climbed up on her back. When they were soaring high, Pena looked at Warrior.

"You are well, my child?" She told him she was better for being here today, and for having him close. "You have always been so close to my heart, like one of my own. You are marrying a great man today. You know that, don't you?"

"I do. I love him with all my heart, and I couldn't have asked for a better man in my life." Warrior nodded and lay down as well. "Have you talked to your son lately? I've heard that he is still having a wonderful time visiting places. I had hoped that he'd be here today too."

"He would have, had he been able. But the place he is at now is remote. But they send their love to you. And a bit of magic that will be with you forever." She and her sister had been made immortal by the magic of the McCades. It was nice to know that she'd live for a long time, but also scary. "You will have many children, won't you? Vance and his wife, they are happy to have a grandchild soon."

"So they've been telling us." She laughed and sat down on his great claw. "I came out here to tell my parents what I thought of them. To tell them that I'm marrying today. That I've never been happier. But once I was here, seeing this place,

I think my heart is as black as the earth that holds them. Not for anyone but them, of course. But as Kerrie pointed out, they'd not care anyway."

"Nay, they would not." She looked up to see her sister and Prisane having a good time. "She has needed to get out of the cave for some time now. I thought today would be a wonderful time to do so. To see you married today is a great honor for us dragons."

"Warrior, I've been meaning to ask you—why did you choose to stay as a dragon? I thought for sure, as everyone did, that the two of you would be humans. Or at least look human like. I'm glad that you're a dragon, but why?" He laughed a little and she felt silly. "I guess it's none of my business."

"Oh, but it is, my child. It's everyone's business that has been in love or falls in love. We decided, while we waited for the magic to consume us, that we'd be dragons for two reasons. One, I've been her dragon for so very long, and she was never one. It was in her heart to fly the skies with me as she once did upon my back." She asked him what the second reason was. "To have hatchlings. We so wanted to have our own children, dragons that would be there for us when we were too old to fly. As humans we would have had children, but it meant so much more to us to bring more of our kind into the world. And to raise them to be the best that they could be. Besides, I think there are enough McCades around that we did not need to add to it."

They were both laughing when her sister joined them. She was windblown, but in high spirits. Prisane laid down again when Kerrie got off her back and ran to the little lake that was nearby. The large dragon looked at the spot where the earth was scorched.

"Don't." She raised her head up to look at her, a smile there in her eyes. "Don't make the ground better here. I like it just the way it is. I mean, if the earth doesn't care that it's there, then I don't either."

"Your sister wishes to plant a tree in their honor. Does that bother you?" Pena told her that while it did a little, she thought it better that she didn't know. "I think she knows more than you think. She is very intelligent, your little sister."

"She is, but I'm not going to ruin her idea of what they were." Prisane nodded. "I'm sorry. But I don't want her to think that she might have been hurt. I'm sure someday that she'll come to me with questions, or to Mom or Dad. But for now, I want to not think about them and what they did. Not today."

"I understand." Prisane had always been her friend, ever since she'd found her near a pond near the castle. "You have only to call to me, my dear, and you know that I'll be there for you. For any of you."

"I know that too. I love you both so very much." She said that she loved her as well. And had a gift for her. "Magic? I don't need anything like that. I'm just happy to be loved by this family."

"Yes, but you will want this. It will help you when you put good use to your studies. It will help you a great deal, as it did the others when you joined them, to be able to read what sorts of things the children have endured." Pena nodded, thinking that would be helpful. "You need only to touch my spike upon my head and it will come to you."

She put her finger on the razor-sharp edge and felt the small pain of it. When the blood welled up, she offered her finger to the dragon. As soon as she licked it clean, she knew that she'd gotten more than the ability to read minds and asked her about it.

"Nothing more than a little magic to help you along the way." Prisane stood up then, and spread her wings. "We must be going now. I'd like to check on my hatchlings before the wedding. You will be a beautiful bride, and he the most handsome of grooms."

Walking back to the house, she saw Mom sitting in the swing that had been built for her long ago. She was simply moving back and forth, but the look on her face looked like she was thinking hard on something. Calling out to her, Mom looked at her and patted the seat next to her.

"I've been thinking." Pena told her that she was thinking too hard. "Yes, more than likely. But I was thinking about the life that you're about to embark on. And I have to tell you, I'm so very proud of you. Of both of you. I never would have thought that you'd be the perfect match. He is somewhat of a serious person."

"Yes, he is at that, but we love each other, and that's about all that matters to me. We balance, he told me." Mom nodded and rocked more. "Are you all right with us marrying? I mean, we sort of jumped the gun by announcing it to everyone before asking."

"Oh my, yes, I'm so very happy. And I cannot wait to be a grandma." Pena pulled out the scale that she'd picked up after Prisane and Warrior left. "You touched it. Do you have any idea what that means?"

"Yes. I do. And I'm sure that he'll be just as happy for us." Her mother nodded and hugged her. "Kerrie wants to plant a tree in the place where they died."

She never referred to them as mom and dad. The only parents she had, as far as she was concerned, were the ones that had loved her and given her a good life. Micky and Vance had given them much more in their first year with them than she'd had her entire young life with the other couple.

"She told me. I cautioned her about things not growing there. But she's set on it. I'll have Vance talk to her about it after the wedding." Mom looked at her. "Speaking of which, I think you need to get ready. You don't have a great deal of time to help me stop crying because my baby girl is leaving me today."

Going into the house, Pena was excited. She was going to be married today, and there wasn't a thing in this world that could dampen her happiness. Pulling on her mom's wedding gown, it all came to her; she was going to be Mrs. Gavin McCade soon.

~~~

Gavin adjusted his tie twice before he pulled it off. Dad came over, took it from him, and put it around his neck. He was nervous and excited, but dad seemed to understand.

"One thing you can be thankful for, she won't have to change her last name." He glared at his dad when he laughed. "Nor will she have to try and get along with her in-laws. There's a lot to be said for marrying someone that you've known for a long time too."

"You're not helping. And we both know that even though we're both McCades, we aren't blood related, not even by marriage." Dad nodded. "Why do I have to wear a tie?"

"Because your bride-to-be is wearing her mom's wedding dress, and you're wearing a tux. Once you are truly wed, then you can toss this off and have fun. But serious stuff has to be done first." Gavin thought of something that had been nagging at his mind for several weeks now. "Don't say it. It doesn't matter."

"I'm over ten years older than her. When she came here, I was already seventeen." Dad said that she'd always be younger than him, but they had lifetimes to be together. "She's so special to me, Dad. I don't want her to regret marrying such an old man."

"Old man? Gavin, you're only thirty-three, not such an old man. And do you have any idea how old Raven is? Or Micky?" He said he was afraid to ask. "Yes, me too. But they're old. Long before we were born they were roaming the earth in search of us. But don't tell them I said they were old. I'm afraid of both of them."

When his tie was fixed, his dad stood next to him in front of the mirror. His dad didn't look that much older than him. He was still as handsome as he was in his wedding pictures that were taken on his wedding day. And his mom, more beautiful than ever before because she loved his dad.

"I have a painting for you and Pena. I took some pictures of the two of you when you joined the family. I painted them side by side like you'd find in a locket. And there is enough

room on it for me to add your children when you have some."
Gavin told him that they were going to have children soon.
"Good. I've never been a grandfather before, and I'm excited
about being one. And I don't have to tell you how excited
your grandma is. It was nice of Pena to ask her to give her
away."

"Grandma has been my best friend and co-conspirator
since I was a kid. I think we got into more trouble than kids
half my age." Dad laughed and said he thought that was true.
"She's going to come and live with us. Did she tell you? Uncle
Vance is happy that she's coming to stay. I was sure that he'd
be upset."

"Why? Everyone knows what she means to the two of you,
especially you. She'll love it there, and you two can get into
more trouble with your wife tagging along. Or, maybe she'll
just stand back with bail money. Could be that is what she'll
do." He laughed, and Dad hugged him. "I'm so very proud of
you, Gavin. And so is your mom. You're a fine attorney now.
Have a nice house and money in the bank. You've taken on
projects that most would just let go. And now you're marrying
a woman that we all love as much as we do you."

"You guys done bonding? Me, I would have thought
you'd done that long ago, but that's just me." Uncle Vance
hugged him too. "Christ, where did the years go? You're all
grown up, and it only seems like yesterday that you were
tugging on my gun belt and asking me to show you how to
toss a knife."

"You explained to me when I had the terminology right,
then you'd show me." Gavin laughed. "I think it took me

208

about a week to figure out what you meant. I'm thankful all the time that you finally did show me how to throw a knife. Some of my clients can be pretty impressed when I do it for them."

The wedding march sounded, and he made his way out to wait on his bride. Pena was his world, and he was excited to be starting this new phase of his life with her. When the bridesmaids finished their walk, he saw her. Pena was the most beautiful creature in the world as far as he was concerned.

Everyone was there. Family, of course, but the dragons had come as well, leaving their hosts, if necessary, to see him getting married. Prisane and Warrior were there as their dragons, providing a beautiful backdrop to the outside wedding.

Faeries and brownies were flittering all over, dropping petals of flowers as Pena and Grandma made their way to him. When he reached for her, Grandma hugged them both tightly, then started to sit. But when she came back, Gavin could hear a few sobs of joy. Grandma told them that she loved them both so much.

Their vows were said to each other, and Gavin realized that his words to her — devotion to her and that he'd love her forever — were sort of lame. Pena cried when he slipped the ring over her finger and he kissed her hand when he did. The minister performing the ceremony said he was just like his father, and they all laughed.

In less time than it took for him to get ready, he was married. And turning his wonderful wife to the crowd of well-wishers, he invited them all to his home for food and fun. Gavin and Pena walked hand in hand to the festivities just as someone called out his name.

"Hello, young man." He hugged Caelin and told him that he didn't think he'd make it. "Miss my own godson's wedding? Never. Besides, your grandma threatened me, so I came. She'd very protective of you, isn't she?"

"She is at that. And I am of her."

They moved with Pena to the party, and Caelin was welcomed like he'd only been away for a few days rather than the last decade. There were many festivities today, and Gavin felt like it was complete. That everyone that he had ever loved was with him on this special day.

Gavin said a small prayer to his grandma, the woman who had cared for him when his mom worked. The faeries had brought her to them and buried her in the most beautiful faerie circle, which he visited weekly.

Someday, he thought, he'd write a book about the dragon warrior and his jewelry. As he walked around, talking to family, he knew he was going to do it. It might not sell well, or not at all, but he was going to write it, because no one would believe what they'd gone through to be a family.

Paranormal Romance with a Bite!

BLOOD, BODY AND MIND:
A KATHI S. BARTON PARANORMAL ROMANCE

YOUR FREE COPY IS WAITING...

Aaron MacManus, the new master vampire of the realm just wanted to go out and meet some of his subjects and to figure out what needed to be done to set things right.

April and Demetrius Carlovetti own an air service and are the most trusted and well liked vampires in Aaron's realm. What he didn't expect when he visited them was betrayal. His own bodyguards try to murder him and blame it on the Carlovetti's.

Sara Temple was not a vampire. She pilots planes for the Carlovetti Airways. She had secrets of her own and working for this small air service is keeping her out of sight. The last thing she wanted to do was save a vampire, even an extremely good looking one.

Sara was only trying to survive but with Aaron she becomes embroiled in politics, the magic of several realms involving a queen in peril, magical beings, passion and love.

Blood, Body and Mind, the first book in the Aaron's Kiss series.

Get Your Free Book!

http://eepurl.com/brCBvP

AWARD WINNING, BESTSELLING AUTHOR

Kathi Barton, winner of the Pinnacle Book Achievement award as well as a best-selling author on Amazon and All Romance books, lives in Nashport, Ohio with her husband Paul. When not creating new worlds and romance, Kathi and her husband enjoy camping and going to auctions. She can also be seen at county fairs with her husband who is an artist and potter.

Her muse, a cross between Jimmy Stewart and Hugh Jackman, brings her stories to life for her readers in a way that has them coming back time and again for more. Her favorite genre is paranormal romance with a great deal of spice. You can visit Kathi online and drop her an email if you'd like. She loves hearing from her fans. aaronskiss@gmail.com.

Follow Kathi on her blog: http://kathisbartonauthor. blogspot.com/